DANGEROUS

BY

SYLVIA MCDANIEL

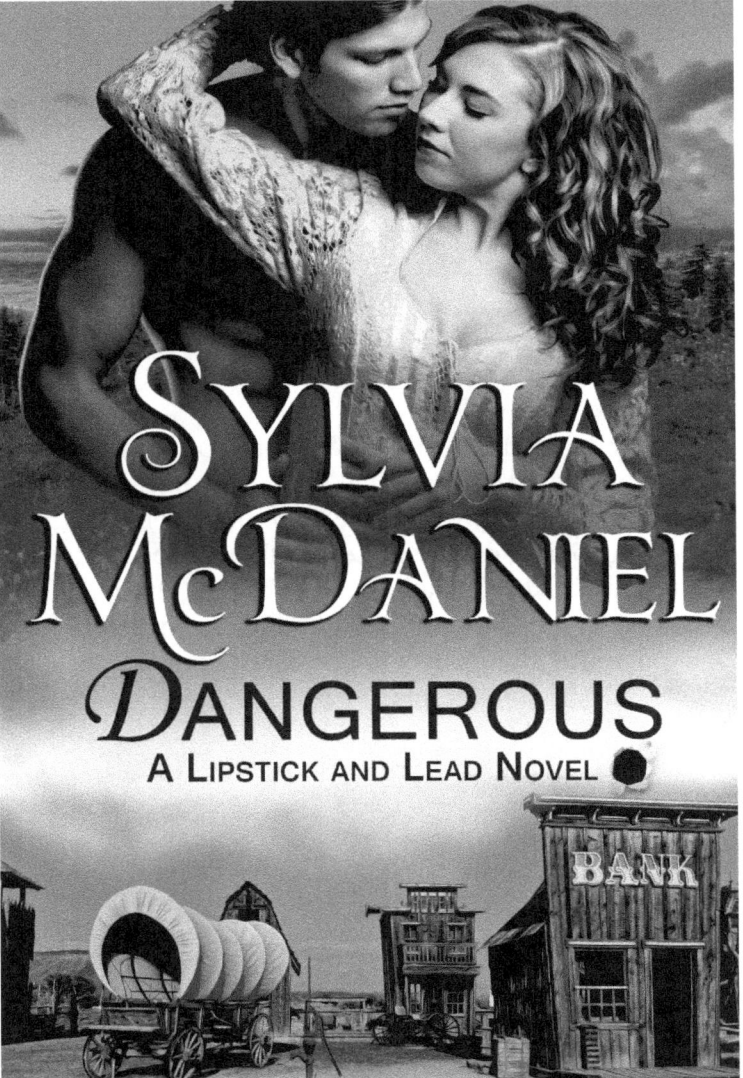

SYLVIA McDANIEL

DANGEROUS

A LIPSTICK AND LEAD NOVEL

They always get their man.

Chapter One

Slap her silly, but she was done! Annabelle McKenzie strode down the wooden sidewalk on her way to the bank. Done with raising chickens, feeding cows and goats, and shoveling manure. She wanted to go with her sisters to hunt for bad men. She wanted to be a bounty hunter.

Deep in thought about how she would explain to her sisters how she craved adventure and longed for excitement, she rounded the corner to enter the bank and slammed into the hard chest muscles of a large dark-haired man. The scent of soap and campfire spiraled straight to her center.

This was a manly man, and Lord knew, they were scarce in Zenith, Texas. Where had this specimen come from?

His hat was pulled low over his face, and he grabbed her by the arms, halting her progress. Her head fit just below his chin. She looked up at his strong, rugged jaw and serious face.

Long black lashes blinked over emerald eyes as he gripped her arms. "Slow down," he said in a deep husky drawl. He kept his head down, barely looking at her.

1

"There's still plenty of cash left in the bank."

What a condescending, egotistical, handsome renegade. Not an "I'm sorry" or "Excuse me", but rather a crass remark about the money in the bank. "Maybe you should watch where you're going."

She tilted her head and stared into his handsome rugged features. There was something about him that seemed familiar, yet she couldn't place him. Somewhere she'd seen his face. She gazed at him. "You're tall enough you should be able to see a woman coming."

He nodded, and she gawked at the way his shirt fit his strong shoulders and muscled arms. His lips were full and tempting, made for kissing.

"You're right, ma'am. I should see a small package like you, barreling around a blind corner. Maybe I need to replace my spectacles with a pair that can see through walls," he said, releasing her arms.

"Maybe you do." The oversized giant was smarting off to her; he wasn't wearing spectacles.

Where had she seen him before? "What's your name?"

A sly smile turned up the corners of his full, luscious lips. "Why? You plan on having me arrested for running into you?"

The man had an ornery mouth, and she was just the woman to give it right back.

"Maybe," she said. "I know the sheriff well. It would serve you right for being belligerent and disrespectful."

He smiled a wickedly sly grin that sent tingles through her. "You have a really *nice* day."

His voice was dripping with sweet sarcasm that made her feel like she'd eaten too many cookies. Tipping his black hat at her, he sauntered out the door.

Like a kick from a bull, it hit her.

His face was on one of the wanted posters she had out in her saddlebags.

For a moment, she stood there stunned, wanting to grab him by the arm and haul him down to the sheriff's office. He was getting away, and yet, part of her wasn't certain he really was a criminal. What if her imagination was stampeding with ideas, trying to keep her from dying of loneliness in this old maid of a town?

But what if this was her chance? Her opportunity to show her sisters she could do more than just watch the cows munch grass. She had bounty hunter blood flowing in her veins. She could catch criminals just as well as they could.

She had two hundred dollars tucked in the satchel on her shoulder. One step closer to paying off the bank note. They only needed a little more, and then the old place would be theirs.

But she didn't have time to make the deposit. She had a criminal to catch.

This morning, she'd stopped at the sheriff's office and picked up the latest wanted posters. Tonight, when she got home, she intended to make her sisters understand. She was nineteen, soon to be twenty, and spent all her life on the farm. She needed to get away from the braying of cattle and the collecting of eggs.

Making a hasty retreat out the door, she watched as the man walked down the street toward the mercantile. Then she hurried to her horse tied up on Main Street.

Opening the leather bags, she thumbed through the papers. The third one she came to had a picture of her man. *Beau Samuel – Wanted for Bank Robbery. Five Hundred Dollar Reward.*

Tingles of alarm galloped along her spine. Oh, my God, she'd just run into him at the bank. He was planning on robbing the Zenith Savings & Loan.

She checked her satchel, finding her six-shooter resting beside her little pot of lipstick. The bounty was more than enough to pay off the bank. Meg could start her dress shop. And Annabelle would have a little adventure in her dull, boring life.

Excitement flooded her nerves like a welcome ray of sunshine. A wide smile spread across her face. This was going to be so much fun. She'd follow Mr. Samuel, and before he left town, he'd be in her custody, and she'd be the heroine who saved the day.

In one afternoon, she would accomplish what Meg and Ruby had taken all year trying to do.

He'd disappeared inside the mercantile. She'd be waiting for him when he came out.

As the family bookkeeper for their bounty hunting business, Lipstick and Lead, it was her responsibility to make certain the bank loan was paid, the farm continued to operate, and supplies were bought, while her sisters had all the fun chasing bad guys and bringing them to justice. Her sisters earned the money, and Annabelle made certain they had a home to return to.

After their father died, they'd learned his profession out of desperation. Bounty hunting paid better than being a waitress or a seamstress or even a housekeeper. And you only had to answer to the men captured and brought to justice.

Not the randy hands of the owner of a business or his employees.

Living on a farm alone, taking care of cattle and chickens and gardening, was enough to make any person

4

question her sanity. In the last year, Annabelle had begun to regret agreeing to take care of their land, while her sisters did the hunting.

She longed for adventure, excitement, danger. Something more challenging than shoveling manure. Only, her sisters disagreed. Meg and Ruby wanted Annabelle to remain on the farm.

Hogwash! It was someone else's turn to babysit the chickens, harvest the garden, and chase the stray cows. Annabelle was about to snag her first bounty.

*

Beau Samuel looked around the mercantile. Quickly, he replenished his supplies and headed out the door. The faster he got out of this one-horse town and circled back to Fort Worth the better. Hopefully, without any run-ins with the law or the Harris gang. That wanted poster was like a rock hanging around his neck. Dangerous and deadly.

One wrong move and he'd find himself in the calaboose.

Opening the door, he stepped around to the back of the building, where he'd tied his horse. The sound of a gun clicking froze his breath in his lungs; his fingers twitched near his sidearm.

"Beau Samuel, you're wanted for robbery."

Sounded like that same aggravating female he'd met at the bank stood behind him with a gun cocked and loaded. He whirled around, grabbed her hand holding the gun, and wrapped his other arm around her, bringing her into his side. "Now, sugar, you know better than to point a gun at a man."

They had a silent tug of war over the gun, and finally, he wrenched the weapon free of her fingers. The sweet scent of roses surrounded the beauty. Her red-gold curls were the type a man would love to run his hands through, but instead, here he was wrestling her for a gun.

What kind of woman was she?

"Damn it," she said. "I'm going to scream my head off, if you don't let go of me and give me my weapon back."

He shoved the gun into his pocket on the other side of his pants, out of her reach. "I wouldn't recommend doing that, unless you want me to silence you with a kiss."

Her blue eyes widened, and she tried to take a step away from him, but he held her firmly in place.

"Besides, I'm not the Beau Samuel that's wanted." He was lying and he didn't care. Why the hell was a woman trying to wrangle him into custody?

"Your face is on the wanted poster."

"It's a mistake," he said, enjoying the feel of her body against his.

"Yeah, and you're a rich cattleman who owns half of Texas. Believe me, I've heard enough tall tales to know when someone's talking out the corner of his mouth. You, sir, are a liar and a thief."

He laughed, gazing down at her, enjoying her pert little nose turned up in a scornful snit. "You get up this morning and have a dose of vinegar to begin your day?"

"Actually, I had two. One is Meg and the other is Ruby."

"Oh, your vinegar has names?" He walked her away from the mercantile. If he could get to his horse, he'd leave this sassy miss behind, after he emptied the chamber of her six-shooter. There was no need for her to put a bullet in him.

"No, they're my bounty hunter sisters, and you're

being served up next."

He laughed. "Sugar, if they are as easy to disarm as you, then you tell them to come on and we'll have a party."

"Oh, it's going to be a party all right." She slapped his hand off her shoulder and wrapped it behind his back, tugging upwards.

She thought she had him in a hold, and he decided to let her think she could get away with it until they reached his horse, Sadie.

"Hey, that hurts," he said, as the woman tugged harder on his arm. It was then that he noticed they were two doors down from the sheriff's office. Dang, now was not the time or the place to draw attention.

Oh no, this wasn't going to happen like she wanted. He had business to attend to that didn't include a stay in the calaboose.

Quickly, he twirled her around, releasing his pent-up arm. Then he slammed her against the outside wall of the bank. Her sapphire eyes widened, and she gazed at him as he leaned into her, not caring that anyone could see them. In fact, he hoped it looked like a lovers' embrace.

"You know, your smart mouth has tempted me all morning. First in the bank and now out on the street. I've taken your gun away. I'm not going to the sheriff's office with you. Now unless you want me to kiss you senseless here in a back alley off Main Street, then I think we need to have a parting of the ways."

She raised her knee and jammed it into his groin, knocking the breath out of him as the world spun crazily, his privates slamming him as pain gripped him, and he gasped for air.

"Damn it," he groaned, slumping over. The woman

packed a nasty punch in that knee.

While he leaned against the wall, gulping for breath, she whispered, "Why would I kiss a man like you, wanted by the law?"

Grabbing his hand, she tried to pull him down the wooden sidewalk. She stopped and considered him. "You're looking a mite peaked."

"Give me a moment. I can't move. You knocked my man parts into next week."

She smiled at him sweetly, and he shook his head. Where in the world had this woman come from and how did he get rid of her? She was trouble and he didn't need the aggravation. He should have been on the road by now.

"You go get the sheriff. I'll wait right here."

"There you go telling tall tales again."

"Does it look like I'm capable of walking right now? Do you think I could get away if I wanted to?" He leaned over and moaned more for effect. The time to leave this town with his hair on was now. He'd be up and on his horse before she could get the sheriff out the door.

Her sapphire blue eyes drew together in a frown. She was a beautiful woman, but he didn't have time to play parlor games. There was a gang hot on his trail. But she appeared to be taking the bait. Just a little bit more and he'd have her on the hook.

"You might have to get me a doctor. I think you broke something."

"Oh, good grief. Stay here and I'll get the sheriff. He can determine if you need a doctor."

He watched her hurry down the back alley. When she got to the door, she stood there for a moment and called into the office.

Beau didn't waste any time. He rose, took the three steps to his horse, and jumped on—pain radiating through him when his crotch met the saddle. Quickly, he pulled out the woman's gun, emptied the chamber and threw the weapon in the dirt where it landed with a thunk.

Good riddance!

Backing up his horse, he turned and galloped down the passageway, making a right at the first street he came too. He'd meander his way through town before taking the road that would get him out of this hellhole.

No wonder that beautiful woman was alone. That sweet face had a tongue that could lash a man into submission or charm him into giving her what she wanted. He needed to put as much distance as possible between them.

Finally, on the edge of town, he kicked Sadie in the sides.

First, the Red River then, the city of Fort Worth—he could only hope he and the Harris gang didn't meet up along the road, or he would be a dead man.

Gigging his horse, he rode at a fast-paced trot. He wanted to put a far piece of trail between him and Zenith, Texas, before the moon rose.

An hour later, shadows fell across the road, and he knew nightfall would soon arrive. He could continue on, but now a gray horse with a woman rode behind him. She'd been back there for over an hour. And every time he glanced back, she appeared a little closer. Could that she-devil be following him on purpose or was it happenstance that they were going the same direction? He turned off the trail behind some trees and waited.

He watched as she turned into the trees. Oh yeah, she

was following him. That she-witch he'd just dumped in town had not given up. That woman had been nothing but trouble. His nuts still ached from the power of her knee. Now he'd have to deal with her again.

*

Annabelle meandered through the trees, leading her horse in the general direction of the ruthless outlaw. What made him decide to get off the trail just as the sun set? Was he making camp for the night or had he spotted her?

She rode along, trying to catch a glimpse of him, but darkness was quickly falling and the idea of sitting in the dark without a fire was not conducive to sleep. Finding Beau Samuel would have to wait until morning.

Pulling her horse to a stop, she slid off and tied him to a tree. In the darkness, she gathered enough wood to last her until morning and set about making a fire.

Their papa had taught them to always carry flint, a few rations, and a canteen of water, but that was all she had. She needed to catch this criminal and get back to town. She wasn't prepared for a lengthy trip.

And Beau certainly hadn't proved to be as easy as she'd thought. She hoped by now she would be home, sitting at the table, telling her sisters all about catching her first bounty. But oh no, they would be worried and angry and frustrated that she hadn't let them know where she was going.

She built up twigs and dried leaves and struck her flint to the material. Soon, she had a roaring fire blazing, casting light. For a moment, she just sat and contemplated her situation.

Maybe she'd left a little too hasty. She had few rations, she had enough money on her to be considered dangerous, and she was following a wanted criminal alone. A dangerous man. A bank robber.

Wouldn't he just love to rob her and leave her dead along the trail?

The brush rustled behind her and she froze. Her heart pounded in her chest, her blood rushing through her. Of all the stupid, rookie mistakes, she realized she'd left her gun in her saddle. No protection, except the small pistol strapped to her pantaloons.

Rising slowly from the ground, she turned and watched as a cotton-tailed rabbit hopped from one bush to the next, hurrying when he saw her standing there.

She breathed a sigh of relief and shook her head. Relaxing would be difficult, but she could expect animal sounds all night long. There was nothing to fear, but she'd get her gun just the same.

Just as she breathed easy, the sound of a gun hammer being drawn back sent terror freezing her lungs as panic pumped her blood.

"You planning on arresting me while I sleep?" a deep voice drawled.

Beau Samuel, bank robber and handsome hunk, breathed in her ear, sending a trickle of awareness through her. Sometimes the best offense was to act dumb.

She whirled around and came face-to-face with the man from the bank. "What are you doing?"

"I'm trying to find out why you're following me. You think you can tie me up and haul me back to town?"

"I didn't know you were out here," she lied. She hadn't heard him sneak up on her, and now she was in a heap of trouble.

"Liar," he said his lips turned up in a smile that any

other time she might have found attractive.

"Where's your good friend the sheriff?"

"We spread out. He should be along any minute now."

"Liar."

"Do you like that word?" She shrugged. "Don't be surprised when the sheriff comes riding in here."

"I just call it like I see it. You're lying. You just don't give up, do you?"

"Why should I?" Annabelle said, staring at him trying to muster courage.

"What's your name Miss Smart Mouth?"

"Annabelle McKenzie, bounty hunter."

He threw back his head and roared with laughter.

"I'm taking you in," she said, incensed that he would laugh at her.

"I outweigh you, I have a gun pointed on you, and I'm stronger than you. Sugar, this is a battle you're not going to win."

"And I'm smarter than you."

He shook his head. "You keep thinking that."

Glancing down at his gun, she looked up at him. "You really think a big strong man like you needs that gun pointed at me?"

"Yeah, I do," he said. "You're dangerous."

"Are you headed to the Red River?" she asked, wanting to know where he was headed in case she lost him. She had no intentions of letting him get away a second time.

"No."

"Then why are you on this road?"

"Lady, it's none of your business why I'm on this road." He shook his head. "Wait a minute. I'm asking the questions, not you."

She smiled at him. When she got away, at least she'd know which direction to follow him.

"I'll just have to go through your saddlebags to see what I can learn about you."

Thank God, she'd strapped the money in a secret pouch inside her skirt. He couldn't find it. If he did, he'd steal it, and then Meg and Ruby would be furious she'd lost some of their bounty money. And she couldn't blame them. They'd worked hard to get the farm out of debt.

"Let me tell you what you're going to find," she said. "Empty bags."

"Liar." He frowned at her.

She shrugged. "Believe what you want. I'd gone into town to buy some supplies. There's nothing in those saddlebags, except for some feminine things I need. Do you understand?"

Come on, she thought, he didn't appear to be that dense.

His eyes widened. "Oh."

"Yes, I thought you wouldn't want to embarrass yourself by going through those rags."

His brow drew together. "Lady, for some reason I think you couldn't tell the truth if it slapped you upside the head."

In two long strides, he reached her horse and drew open the first saddlebag. It contained the wanted posters. *Dang! Dang! Dang!*

Why had she thought this would be so easy?

He pulled them out and his was on top. He held it up. "You know, I don't think the artist caught my best side? Do you?"

She frowned. "He left off your horns."

A smile spread across his face as he laughed and shook his head. "Woman, you have a smart mouth, and it's going to get you killed," he said. "I was hoping you'd learned a lesson this afternoon and wouldn't follow me."

"There's five hundred dollars riding on your head. I'd follow you a long ways trying to earn that cash." That would be the final payment on the farm. They'd be completely debt free and her sisters would no longer have to hunt lawless men.

"Are you hungry? Do you need the money?"

"No," she said, surprised.

"Then why are you out chasing outlaws for money? It seems to me a woman like you would have a husband and a passel of kids by now."

The gun in his hand was pointed at her midsection and that made her uneasy. It could so very easily go off. "Who says I don't?"

He considered her comment, staring at her like he wasn't certain if she was telling the truth or yet another lie. "Is your husband waiting somewhere up the road and together the two of you were going to make some extra cash?"

"Oh, he's waiting somewhere up the road, that's for certain."

The idea sounded good, and if he were stupid enough to believe it, then she'd let him. So far, her luck with men hadn't been good. One wife-cheating restaurant owner and nothing else. Was she ugly as sin or unappealing in some way?

He shook his head. "Why would a man send a woman alone to capture me? None of this makes sense."

She smiled and cocked her head. "Maybe I'm just a lonely woman trying to get home. Maybe I'd forgotten all about our little run-in behind the sheriff's office."

"Liar." He gazed at her, his eyes a deep dark green that shone brightly in the firelight. And those dark lashes, they could flutter and set a girl's heart quivering. "And you're not too good at tall tales."

"Why, thank you. I've never wanted to be known as a woman who could lie well."

God, if she could just get out of this. If she could manage to turn the guns on him, tie him up, then drag him back to Zenith and collect her bounty, she'd never do this again. She'd never thought bounty hunting was easy, but she'd never considered how close, how involved you had to become with the criminal in order to catch them. How risky. Innocently, she'd thought it would be so much simpler. Birthing a calf was easier than catching a criminal, though probably messier.

She'd leave bounty hunting to Meg and Ruby and go back to taking care of cows. Smelly, stinking, mooing cattle, who didn't have the sense to get out of the rain.

"So, what's it going to be, sweetheart? Are you going to tell me the truth or am I going to have to beat it out of you?"

Beat it out of her? Really? Of course, he was a wanted outlaw. A dangerous man who could hurt her. But then again, was he just trying to scare her? Inside, she was quaking, but she was determined to appear as if she wasn't worried.

"Tell me about the beating. What exactly would you do to me? Not that I'm lying to you, but I'm just considering all my options here." She hoped he was trying to intimidate her and wasn't serious about harming her. From their interaction, he seemed more of a smart aleck than a truly evil man.

He frowned at her and shook his head. Taking a step toward her, he stood close enough she was forced to look up. "Lady, I should have known you were going to be trouble when I ran into you at the bank."

"Did you rob that bank?" she asked.

"Hell, no."

"Are you planning on robbing the bank?"

"There you go again, asking the questions. I'm in charge here. I'm the one with a gun pointed at you. I'm threatening to beat you."

Yeah, he was threatening to beat her, but he really didn't seem the type. For an outlaw, there was something oddly decent about him.

She shrugged. "I just wanted to know the answer to my questions. I mean, you're wanted for robbing a bank. You could have been scouting our little bank. I have money in there. I may need to withdraw it all before I see you in town again."

He shook his head. "Answer my question."

"Could you repeat the question? I've forgotten it since we started talking."

"Why are you following me?"

"Simple. Five hundred dollars. You're my bounty."

He didn't respond, but grabbed her arm and then dragged her over to his waiting horse. With the gun still pointed on her, he reached inside and pulled out some rope.

"What are you doing?" she asked, a feeling of unease skittering down her spine, wondering what he intended to do with the rope.

He didn't say a word, but shoved his gun into his holster and spun her around like she was a spindle top, tugged her arms behind her back, and tied her wrists together.

"Why are you tying my hands? It's very uncomfortable." This wasn't good. This wasn't good at all. She needed her hands available to fight him off. To get to her gun. To escape and return with her sisters. She should have gotten Ruby and Meg before coming out on this trip.

"I'm not interested in your comfort."

"Why are you so mean? Are you proving to me that you can be a bad guy?"

Beau stopped and looked at her. A smile lifted one corner of his mouth. "Sugar, I don't have to prove anything. I know I'm one mean son of a bitch. And you want to take me into the sheriff. Did you think I was going to faint and say please take me to my hanging?"

She shook her head. "A girl can hope."

He chuckled then reached down and traced his finger along her mouth. "You've got one smart mouth."

A shiver trickled down her spine, igniting areas of her body in a way she'd not experienced before. She didn't know if it was fear or some other emotion she hadn't yet identified.

How was she going to get out of this while she was tied up? She'd left a note in the sheriff's office when she'd gone in to get Zach, but he was long gone and the office was empty for the day. Hopefully, he would be on his way here in the morning. She would do her best to ride this out until then.

Beau didn't say a word but marched her back to the campfire. "Get comfortable. It's going to be a long night."

"I need a bedroll."

He glanced over at her horse. "You don't have one?"

"No, but you do," she said with a smile.

"Who rides out without a bedroll? Do you have any supplies? Anything?" he asked, staring at her like she was crazy.

"Yes, I've got a few supplies."

"You followed me on a whim. Greenhorn mistakes like that can cost you your life."

"I'm not a greenhorn," she spit out.

"Well then, you're not very smart."

Annabelle had to bite her lip to keep from saying anything. She'd followed him without much thought as to her actions. Maybe it wasn't the smartest thing she'd ever done, but he'd have to torture her before she'd ever admit to her error.

He got up, marched over to his horse, and pulled off his bedroll. He came back to the fire and spread it out. "We'll share."

"No. We won't."

"Your husband wouldn't approve?" he said with a mocking smile.

This had just gotten way more serious than she'd anticipated. She'd never considered the danger to herself, only the reward when she brought in her captive.

"Lay a hand on me and my husband will beat you until you're talking out of the other side of your mouth." She sat on the ground, facing him, watching his every move. "I don't care where you sleep. I'm taking the bedroll."

He stared off into the night, a wrinkled crease on his forehead, like he was deep in thought. Suddenly, he grabbed her hand and held it up to the firelight. She watched with trepidation as his lips curled in a smile. "I don't think you're married. There's no ring. No shadow of a former ring. There's no man waiting down the road for you. You're alone."

"Not for long. My sisters are on their way, and they'll be bringing the law."

"Well then, I'll be sure to leave you tied up where they can find you."

"You wouldn't."

"I would." He leaned back against his saddle, closed his eyes and pulled his hat low. "Good night, bounty hunter."

"You bastard."

He chuckled. "Such a nasty, sassy mouth. Makes me want to kiss it and make it sweeter."

Chapter Two

The sound of horses' hooves pounding on the nearby road woke Beau. The sun was just beginning to peek over the eastern sky, chasing the shadows from the earth. Slowly, he got to his feet and edged the fifty yards closer to the road, peering into the gloom. Six riders of the Harris gang sat astride their horses, not far from where he stood.

He held his breath, hoping the woman he'd left back at camp would still be sleeping and would remain silent. He held his breath, hoping the coals from the fire had died enough no smoke was visible. He held his breath, knowing if they found him, they'd want answers about the bank robbery money.

"Give me a minute," Jake said, leaning over his horse. "I'm feeling sick."

Beau watched the gang member vomit in the road. The cruel group of men laughed at the longrider as he spewed his guts.

"He's so drunk he couldn't hit the ground with his hat in three tries," William said with an ugly laugh. In the gloomy light of dawn, the leader's eyes were dark and menacing in a way that sent tingles of warning up Beau's spine. William was a cold-hearted killer who would shoot a man for very little cause. Just like Beau's older brother had no remorse about killing innocents.

"I'm fine," Jake slurred. "I'll just hang onto my horse, and she'll follow you guys wherever it is we're going."

They must have spent the night in town, drinking and gambling and whoring. A normal night's activity for these ruffians. An exercise in depravity Beau had watched over the last few months.

"Not good enough. You're slowing us down," William said, as he spat on the ground. "You're a drunk, Jake. You're dangerous and you're going to get one of us killed."

The man frowned and stared at William like he wanted to argue the point. "We're all drunk. I'm not the only one."

"Yes, you are. Dan, are you drunk?"

"No way."

"Tom, are you drunk?" William asked.

"Nope."

That tingle crawling up Beau's spine suddenly felt like a raging river of warning, and he shrank further behind the brush, praying Annabelle would keep quiet.

William turned to the man in the middle. "Grant, are you drunk?"

"No."

"Jim, are you drunk?" he asked the man beside him.

"Not anymore."

They all turned their attention back to Jake, and there was a dangerous undercurrent Beau could feel from twenty feet away.

"Every time we get ready to do a job, you get drunk,

Jake."

The man swiped his face with his hand as if to clear the alcohol from his brain. "No, I don't. I just like to have a little whiskey the night before to get my courage up."

William shook his head, his eyes darkened and his mouth curled in a snarl. "You don't have a little whiskey. It takes a whole stinking bottle before you find any courage."

The men laughed and Beau knew the boy was in trouble. He had to help him, but how? His mind churned furiously, wondering if he could distract the ruthless gang.

"One drink turns into two and soon the bottle is gone," Jake said, clearly realizing the danger he was in. "I won't do it anymore. I promise."

"Your drunk ass slows us down, your hands shake, and you stink. I've had enough." William whipped out his pistol and shot the man before he had a chance to respond.

Beau jumped inside his skin, too late to help the poor bastard. The blast of the gun echoed through the trees, the boom loud enough to send birds fluttering from their perches. If that hadn't woken the girl, then she could sleep through a thundering herd of cattle.

Thank God, she hadn't screamed.

Jake's body hit the ground with a splat. His horse neighed nervously and sidestepped away from the dead man.

The outlaws stared at the man on the ground and then looked at their leader. No one said anything, knowing they'd be next if they protested. Beau had ridden with these men, and they were a ruthless bunch, but their leader was as cold-blooded as a rattler with a chill.

"Tom, pull his body off the trail and let's get going. We need to find Beau and get our money. We're not far behind him, so he can't be much further. And if any of the rest of you feel the need to drink yourself silly the night before we ride, keep in mind what happened to Jake."

Tom jumped down from his horse and pulled Jake's body into the woods. Beau watched as the hold-up man stepped back into his stirrups. Then the group swiftly rode away, leaving the dead man.

Beau's heart galloped like a racing horse as he watched the backs of the gang disappear over the hill. Eventually, they'd find him, and once they did, William would require answers to the question as to where he'd hidden the money. And if Beau was lucky, they'd let him live.

Quickly, he crossed the road and felt Jake's pulse. Dead. Definitely dead.

With a sigh, he realized he couldn't leave the girl behind. He couldn't ride off and let her face the Harris gang tied up and helpless. Now he would be saddled with the responsibility of a mouthy woman, a wanted poster, locating the robbery money, and the need to reach Fort Worth.

*

Annabelle couldn't feel her hands any longer. The sound of a gunshot had startled her out of a deep sleep. The first restful moment she'd had all night. The boom of the gun had frightened her, especially when she opened her eyes to a cold campfire and no Beau. After a long, anxious night, that no-good badman had gone off and left her alone, with her hands tied behind her back. Helpless.

And Annabelle hated the feeling of having no control.

A crunch of a twig alerted her that someone approached. Troubled, she jumped and rolled to a sitting position. Beau stepped into camp.

"Where the hell have you been? Did you hear that gunshot? Was that you? You go off and leave me tied up, alone without the benefit of a weapon?"

There was a coldness about his face that was disturbing this morning. His emerald gaze fell on her and his brows rose in a mocking glance.

"Good morning, Miss Mary Sunshine. How are you feeling?" he asked, his voice all fake cheery. "Was the hotel bedding up to your standards?"

If her hands hadn't been tied, she would have shown him exactly how she was feeling, and it wasn't pretty. Her hair was hanging down, her hands ached, and she'd slept very little. She missed her bed. "I can't feel my hands. They're numb."

"Let me untie you. Then you go and do whatever it is women do first thing in the morning. As long as you're nice. No tricks."

She snorted as he stepped over to her and helped her to stand. Then he began untying the ropes that held her wrists. "Don't go far. There were riders out on the road this morning."

"My sisters?" she asked hopefully.

"No, the Harris gang," he said quietly, his voice more serious than the moment before. "They're some mean hombres."

"How do you know them?" she asked.

He sighed, the sound heavy in the stillness of the dawn. "God, woman, you are full of questions. Just do

24

what I say."

The outlaw was certainly not a bright and early kind of guy. He was a grump of the worst sort this morning. But she wasn't going to let that trouble her. She didn't care what kind of mood he was in. She needed an explanation of how he knew the outlaws, and she wanted to go home. Preferably with him tied up and riding behind her.

"I want answers."

"And I want gold. Hope you get what you want."

Aargh, he was the most infuriating man she'd ever met. Even more than that worthless man specimen she'd worked for as a waitress. Were all men a pain?

He finished untying the ropes. Needles tingled as the blood flowed slowly back into her wrists and her fingers. She moved her shoulders as she clenched and unclenched her hands. When she thought she had enough feeling back in them, she swung her fist at his head. He caught it in mid-air.

"What are you doing? I said no tricks. Do you want me to tie you back up?" he asked, his brow drawn together in a frown.

"Trying to pay you back for tying me up and then leaving me alone. You scared me and I don't scare easily," she said, stepping to within inches of him, staring into his gaze.

The corner of his mouth lifted in a curl. "Well, I didn't think you wanted to go to the bushes with me, but next time I'll be sure to take you. As for tying you up, I like sleeping without worrying that you're going to hornswaggle me while I rest. Now, are you going to behave yourself and go do your business or do I need to go with you? I'd be happy to help."

"Just let me go," she said, knowing she sounded as dejected as she felt.

Annabelle was worn out. What had she been thinking to follow this outlaw out of town, instead of going home and telling her sisters they were missing a bounty? But oh no, she'd thought this would be so simple she'd be home before suppertime with the money to pay off the bank loan.

Now her sisters would be worried sick and furious when they learned the truth. And Annabelle would gladly sit at home and watch the chickens scratch in the dirt, where she belonged. Not sleeping out in the country, going hungry, and riding until the muscles in her buttocks screamed enough.

"Go do your business," he said softly and gave her a little push on the back.

But most of all, she was scared of Beau Samuel. While he seemed a nice enough man, he was a criminal—a thief who'd robbed a bank and obviously had no wish to die of throat trouble by hanging from a tree.

She turned and glared at him. "Paws off, mister."

"Then go do what you're told."

"No one tells me what to do," she said defiantly. Right now, she just wanted to irritate him as much as she felt frustrated by her own silly mistake.

"We're breaking camp in less than five minutes. You can either go to the bushes or you can hold it all day. I don't care. Your choice." He turned and started to pack his saddlebags.

She frowned, suddenly realizing he intended for her to go with him. Last night, he'd said he would leave her tied up where her sisters would find her. What had changed and why? "I'm not going with you."

This morning he seemed tense, unlike yesterday. For a moment, he didn't say anything but continued to roll up the bedroll. He kicked dirt over the fire and tried to erase signs of their camp. She watched him, studying his actions.

"You don't want the Harris gang to find you?" she asked.

"You've got four minutes before I put you on your horse and we roll out of here."

"I'm not going with you," she said again, her voice rising. He was going to make her go with him to keep his location a secret. What had she gotten herself into? She just wanted to go home.

"Sugar, I tried to get you to not follow me. Now, I have no choice, but to take you with me."

"No. I'm not going."

He looked up at her from tightening the cinch on his saddle. "I'm not leaving you here alone, with the Harris gang searching for me. Not unless you want to be the center of their attention, and I don't think you really do. But then again, Miss Sassy Mouth, you may enjoy the attentions of more than one cowboy at once. Maybe you like being treated like a whore."

Her mouth dropped open at the realization of what he was telling her. Her breath froze in her lungs as her eyes widened. She licked her lips rapidly and swallowed. "Just let me ride back to Zenith. I know the way."

She was less than a day's ride away from home. She could be home by suppertime, tell her sisters what they needed to know about Beau, and once again take up her role as head bookkeeper, farmer, and chicken wrangler.

His expression was one of sympathy and that

frustrated her even more. Because she knew, he would force her to go with him.

"Again, that gang is going to be circling back. A woman alone on the trail would be like Christmas and the fourth of July arrived on the same day for them. And from the looks of what they did to that feller across the clearing, you'd be pushing up daisies when they were done with you."

She stammered, her pulse racing as realization smacked her in the gut. "That shot...that shot this morning was them killing a man?"

His face tightened, his mouth drawing into a frown as his eyes darkened and something painful lingered for a moment in his gaze.

"Yes, you've got two minutes before we leave. When we find a farmhouse, I'll leave you behind with a farmer and his wife, but don't go riding off alone. A pretty woman like yourself would be like candy to starving men."

He'd called her pretty. She swallowed and knew she had no choice. Her adventure would continue. "I'll be quick."

"Good girl. As soon as you're done, we ride."

Annabelle found her a bush and quickly finished her business. Of all the stupid things she'd ever done in her life, leaving town without her sisters was the biggest mistake she'd made. And now she was riding off with an outlaw to escape more outlaws and hoping Meg and Ruby were on their way to rescue her. Hoping her beloved sisters didn't run into the Harris gang.

Quickly, she drew an A in the dirt, praying they'd see it.

*

"Where are we going?" Annabelle asked as they rode north toward the hidden money. Beau needed to keep the Harris gang guessing as to his original destination, but he knew they were all headed to the same location.

"I think I'm going to have to limit the number of questions you ask each day. Maybe then my poor ears will get a rest," he said, teasing her, enjoying the way she bantered with him.

She was a lively filly with a womanly figure that had caught his attention when he first laid eyes on her. He wondered how his hands would fit around her waist and how she would feel snug against his body or how her full lips would taste beneath his own. Those were things a man was better off not thinking about. But with this slip of a woman, it was damn hard not to.

"I'm smart enough to know we're headed north. But there are not many towns in this direction."

He hadn't tied her hands again, after seeing how much they'd hurt after he'd released her. He'd never thought about the circulation being cut off, but only how he could keep from waking up in the middle of the night with her standing over him with a gun in her hand. The woman was damn fine looking but crazy as a loon to be chasing after bad guys alone.

"You're right."

"Aren't you going to tell me anything else?" she asked, clearly frustrated with him.

He let her stew for a moment or two. "We've been zigzagging. Never going in one direction for too long, hoping that if someone followed us, we'd lose them."

No, he wasn't a bad guy, but she didn't know that. She didn't know he was just a sheep in wolf's clothing trying to right a wrong. Yet, he liked the idea of her

29

playing Little Red Riding Hood. To his hungry eyes, she looked mighty tasty.

"Even my sisters."

"Anyone."

After he'd told her about the dead man across the road, she'd promised him she'd behave as long as he didn't tie her hands. And so far, she'd kept her word. But he had a sneaky suspicion that sometime today, before nightfall, she'd pull some kind of trick. And he'd be prepared.

"You know my sisters are on their way."

"Sugar, I'm terrified."

"You should be."

Three women did not frighten him. Still, he'd rather be traveling alone. Annabelle slowed him down and was a nuisance, and yet, he didn't mind gazing at her. She was an excellent horsewoman and knew how to ride without sitting in one of those side saddles.

When he looked at her skirt, he saw it was full enough she could sit a horse and have her skirts billowed around her, covering all but the tops of her ankles, which her boots hid.

No, she was all wrapped up like a proper lady, yet she wasn't one of those pampered women who fainted at the mere mention of an improper word.

"Again, Mr. Samuel, where are we going?"

The woman had grit. And he admired that about her. Annabelle McKenzie could hold her own and curse as unexpected as a fifth ace in a poker deck. Stubborn, mule-headed, mouthy, and a pain in his ass were also words to describe her pretty little self.

He shook his head, knowing this was going to be a long day, unless he found a farmer soon. The quicker, the better. But even as they wandered in the wilderness, like the Israelites, off the main trail, it was hard to find civilization. So far, they'd ridden the better part of the day and had no sight of anyone other than themselves and a few startled deer.

"Sugar, the less you know the better, unless you enjoy five randy outlaws."

She flashed her bluebonnet eyes at him like she was setting the prairie ablaze. "Would you please stop saying that? If you're doing it to scare me, it worked. I'm here, aren't I? It's losing its effectiveness. Now, it's just making me mad. So mad that if they rode up this moment, I'd probably kill the whole lot of them and you as well."

He laughed. "Well, I guess mad is better than scared. But I'm still not telling you where we're going. And I've never seen a woman who could fire a gun well enough to kill a man, especially one without a pistol."

"Then you haven't seen my sisters and me. Our papa taught us how to protect ourselves. Anytime you want to contest me in a shooting match, I'm game."

If he were a betting man, he'd guess that somewhere on Miss Annabelle McKenzie there was a hidden pistol. Somewhere beneath all those lacy petticoats, she was concealing a weapon. And he couldn't blame her. A pretty woman like her needed protection.

"Well, I will certainly keep that in mind. Don't want to make you angry enough to become a free lunch for the coyotes."

"Hrmph," she said, her blue eyes raking him.

Most women would have been fussing about the pace they were riding, but so far she'd kept up with him. She hadn't even complained when they'd ridden through some tall brush. Her dappled gray mare had a blaze of white on its face, and she controlled that filly with excellent horsemanship. Better than any woman he'd ever seen ride and even a lot of men, but still she was a woman.

And he needed to find a farmhouse and leave her behind, before his thoughts got him into all kinds of trouble that he didn't need.

"What can you tell me about the sheriff in Zenith? You said you knew him."

"I do. He's sweet on my sister, but why should I tell you anything? You're not sharing information, so why should I?"

Beau shook his head. "This is why women should stay at home."

She glanced over at him, sending him a look that could have singed his shirt and pants. And maybe even his skin too.

"Stay home and do what?"

"Raise children, run a home, cook for their family."

Annabelle pulled on her reins, leading her horse around a cedar bush that was over six feet tall. When their horses came back together side by side, her blue eyes narrowed at him.

"And what happens to a woman when her man, who brings in all the money, dies? Who takes care of her and the children then? Do you think she'll be able to go out and earn as much money as her husband was making?" she asked.

He shrugged. "I don't know. I guess I never thought much about it."

Somehow he'd found a touchy nerve. Her feelings were hemorrhaging, running her mouth like a doctor with a bunch of leeches.

"And if she does find a job, do you know what she'll have to put up with?"

"No," he said quietly, knowing that she would soon tell him.

"Let's just say I'd have probably ended up in jail if I'd had to remain a waitress much longer. Some man would have placed his hands in the wrong spot, and I would have blown out his lamp permanently."

He laughed, suddenly understanding what had caused that sore spot. A cowboy had undoubtedly played fast and loose with the waitress. And yet, he had a sudden urge to pulverize the man for causing Annabelle to suffer. "I guess you don't have many suitors."

She stopped and gave him a look that was both haughty and disdainful. "No. I don't. A strong woman needs an even stronger man. I haven't met one yet I thought was a catch."

Guiding his horse around an oak tree, he glanced over at her and smiled. "That almost sounds like a challenge. Do you think I'm a tough man?"

"You're an outlaw. You rob banks for a living and prey on the weak. You may be physically brawny, but I also want a man who is powerful in character. You're damn weak." A frown drew between her brows, like it hurt to think.

People always had thought badly about him, once they learned who his family was. He could be a saint, but the taint from his blood would darken his reputation.

"Hey, you don't know that," he admonished.

She glanced over at him, her eyes mocking. "If you were strong of character, then why aren't you making a living without being a thief?"

He closed his eyes and kept his mouth shut. He couldn't say a word. He couldn't explain to her that none of this was his fault.

"Some things can't be helped," he said quietly.

God, she was a daunting woman, and he liked that about her even more. Years had passed since he'd met a woman he was intrigued enough to pursue. One that was his equal.

Who knew what she wanted? Whatever it was, Annabelle had the guts and the determination to go after her desires.

"So, what do you want in life, Miss Smart Mouth?"

She gazed at him like he'd taken a wrong turn in a cattle drive and was leading her over a cliff.

"A man who will give me his heart and be by my side until I take my last breath. A couple of kids and a nice farm to raise them on. Somewhere that's peaceful and quiet. Not an outlaw."

He nodded his head and wiped the sweat from the back of his neck. The spring day was hot and humid, like the air was saturated with moisture.

"Doesn't seem like you're asking for a lot." Desolation descended on him. Of all the places for him to meet a woman who grabbed his fancy, now was not the time. He needed his wits about him, just to keep them both alive.

"You wouldn't think so, but sometimes the simplest things are the hardest to achieve."

"I agree." Not only hard, but he reckoned a good home was impossible for him.

They rode along in silence, her brow furrowed as if she was deep in thought. Somehow, he had a suspicion that couldn't be good for him. What kind of trouble was brewing in that head of hers?

"What part do you have the hardest time attaining?" he asked.

She frowned. "That's a little personal."

"Just asking, trying to pass the time. Do you have a farm?"

"Yes, it belongs to my sisters and me."

"We've already established that you have no man," he said with a laugh.

If she could have reached him, she probably would have hit him. Her blue eyes glared at him. It didn't take a college degree to know he wouldn't be sleeping on the blanket if they were still together tonight.

She led her horse across a small stream and into a wide-open field. "Do we have to talk about this?"

He glanced around, scanning the open area and the hills on either side, and laughed. "There's the problem. You can't find a man."

"No. Not many men in town want anything to do with the McKenzie sisters."

"Why not?" he asked, noticing the clouds were starting to build in the west like a dust storm from a raging herd of runaway cattle. They were white, but almost churning like boiling water in the sky. Springtime in Texas. Cold one minute, warm the next with raging storms between.

"Now you're asking a lot of questions."

He smiled and glanced around the countryside looking for anything that moved or a farmhouse. Leaving her behind with a farmer would be safer for him and for her. But he hadn't seen a farm yet.

She sighed. "We're not exactly the prim and proper, mild-mannered women that most men are seeking. Meg has worn pants all her life, though she can turn burlap into a ball gown. And then there's Ruby—wild, wicked, and spontaneous. Since she almost killed that Clay Mullins kid, no man has come near her. I think she prefers it that way. I worry about her. She's no longer an innocent, doe-eyed young woman. And she takes way too many risks."

Inside he was trying not laugh. The descriptions of her sisters would send any man running. A house filled with strong-headed, beautiful women, if they looked like her, and three sassy mouths. A smart man would run in the opposite direction. No wonder she'd been unable to find a man to marry her.

"It's probably better that Ruby has toughened up. Especially if she's out chasing men wanted by the law," he said, wondering about the sisters. He'd heard rumors that there were women collecting bounties, but he'd blown the gossip off as dime-novel fiction. Maybe it was true.

"Yeah, anyway, the town has no respect for three women who don't follow the rules."

He nodded his head, a smile spread across his face. "What about you? You didn't describe your part in gaining a reputation. What did you do?"

For a moment, he watched as she considered his question. "Nothing. I'm probably the tamest of my sisters—or at least I was until this trip."

Oh no, he wasn't buying that. If she was considered mild mannered or meek next to her sisters, then Lord help any man who tangled with these she-wolves.

"I think you outdid yourself this time. What were you thinking coming after a known criminal? What if I was a killer? I could have murdered you and left you for dead."

"Hey, I'm not that easy to take on," she said, her voice rising petulantly.

"Sugar, you weren't too hard to sneak up on either, were you?"

She drew herself up in the saddle, her eyes flashing with enough spark and sizzle to set the woods on fire. "Look, I may not be as savvy as my sisters when it comes to this bounty hunting business, but I knew how to handle men in the restaurant. They thought I was one of the side dishes, and some of them went away wearing their dinner."

The image of Annabelle dumping a plate full of food on some poor fool was enough to make him smile. He'd have to be careful around food with her. Wearing his dinner would make him a little perturbed with the beauty.

Annabelle turned in her saddle and stared at him, her voice rising with emotion. "I just want to help my sisters. And I wanted to get away from watching the grass grow for a while. Do you know what's it like to be alone day in and day out? It gets boring. I found myself talking to the chickens. The *chickens*," she said with emphasis.

He laughed. "I know. When I spend weeks out on the trail looking for a man, it can get pretty darn lonesome. You're glad to reach a town and get to talk to people again, until they learn who you are."

The trail was a lonely place. Even though he enjoyed tracking, it got old. Real old. Especially when the weather turned bad, like now. A storm was brewing.

She stared at him her gaze questioning. "What man were you looking for?"

He realized he'd told her more information than he wanted her to know. "Occasionally, I'll do a job for the gang and hunt a man, especially if he owes money. I find him and collect."

A frown flitted across her face, and she shook her head. "Liar. I think they'd want you to kill him."

The woman was too damn perceptive. She was a nice little filly that he wouldn't mind taking to the pasture for a tryout. But dang it, no one had accused Beauregard Samuel of killing men without them taking it to the street.

"No, I've never killed a man in cold blood. Never." That was something he wouldn't lie to her about. He wanted her to feel safe, not just safe enough to stay.

Dark angry clouds rolled against the sky as the sun disappeared. Springtime in Texas meant rain, thunder, and often high winds. Looked like they were soon to learn what the elements had in store for them.

"I think it's going to rain." She glanced worriedly at the sky.

"Let's see if we can find a place to get out of the weather. There are some caves in this area. Be on the lookout." He'd hidden in one in this area before.

"Caves?"

"Yeah, we can build a fire and stay nice and dry tonight." Maybe she'd even let him share the blanket with her.

"What about bats?" she asked, her blue eyes wide with fear.

"What about them?"

"Won't they be in the caves?"

"Yes, but they won't bother us as long as we leave them be."

She shivered. "They have weird eyes. They have bugs and diseases."

Finally, he'd found something the woman feared.

Finally. "Just ignore them."

Thunder rumbled low and distant, reminding them they were running out of time.

"Bats are creepy," she said, glancing around the countryside. "Wish I was back home in Zenith."

Me too, Beau thought. Annabelle McKenzie was an interesting woman who could get under his skin way too easy. Her tough spirit was fun to rouse. He wondered how her full lips would taste and feel like beneath his.

He needed to leave her behind at a farmhouse quick, before she reminded him of the life he'd given up.

Chapter Three

Ruby wanted to pace the small house, but the weather was changing, and her ankle had swollen again. Over a month had passed since the accident that took her off the trail of Simon Trudeau and locked her inside this house with Annabelle, until she and her sister had gone after Meg.

Annabelle had never been on a hunt before, and for the first time in her life, she'd experienced the thrill of the chase.

Now, Meg had disappeared while Ruby had been in the barn, and Annabelle hadn't come home from town yesterday. Ruby was worried sick something had happened to both her sisters, though they were quite capable of defending themselves. Knowing Annabelle, anyone who messed with her would be so full of holes he wouldn't even float in brine. Yet, Ruby would have ridden to town after her if she weren't sitting here waiting on Meg.

"Where is everyone? I walk out to the barn and everyone disappears," she said out loud to herself.

Tomorrow morning, she would saddle up her Mustang and ride to town. Both women missing worried her.

And of all the lousy luck, her ankle was choosing this moment to swell up fatter than a Christmas hen.

She was ready to get back to doing what she loved. Bounty hunting. Catching bad men and bringing them to justice. She was ready to ride the trail again.

The door swung open, and Meg walked in, grinning like a possum eating a yellow jacket, her cheeks blushing and green eyes bright and shiny.

"Where have you been?" Ruby said, trying to stand, so put out with her sister she wanted to whack her upside the head.

Zach Gillespie walked in behind her, his lips stretched across his face like he'd won the grand prize at the county fair.

Oh, God!

"What's going on?" Ruby asked, a suspicious feeling skittering down her spine. "Last I saw you, Meg, you were ready to tie him to the hanging tree."

"Now, Ruby, we were both mad." Meg glanced at the tall, dark-haired man with earthy brown eyes, her cheeks blushing.

Her tall red-haired sister never blushed. Never.

Meg's mouth was red and swollen like she'd been kissing, but Meg also liked to put a little paint on her lips to give them that rich color.

"We've worked out our differences. Where's Annabelle? We want to tell you both the news at the same time."

"I can already see what's coming." Ruby shook her head. "I thought Annabelle was with you. She's not come home since yesterday. She rode out to the bank and then you disappeared. I've been sitting here worried sick about both of you, wondering when you were going to come home."

Meg frowned and stared at Zach, her green eyes suddenly anxious. "We haven't seen her. We...we went to see the Reverend and then straight to the hotel."

Ruby shook her head, knowing without being told what going to the Reverend's had entailed. "You married him."

A smile crossed Meg's face, and she placed her arm inside Zach's. "Yes, we got married."

Zach grinned like a jackass eating cactus. He wrapped his arms around Ruby's sister, holding her tight. "Once she agreed, I wasn't letting her out of my sight again. Nothing was going to stop us from finding the sin-buster and saying I do."

Meg stared all doe-eyed at the sheriff like he'd sprouted a halo. "And he rented us a place in town, where I can have my dress shop downstairs and we can live above."

Ruby frowned as a trickle of unease wound its way up her spine like a spider spinning a sticky web. "That's great, but what about Lipstick and Lead? How are we going to pay off the bank note?"

Ruby wasn't ready to sit at home on the farm. She enjoyed being a bounty hunter, and she'd take this life over being a maid or housekeeper any day.

"Once I get the dress shop going, we won't need Lipstick and Lead any longer. You girls can work the farm, I'll run my dress shop, and Zach will be the sheriff."

Meg was fulfilling her dream, and Ruby was happy for her sister, but that wasn't Ruby's dream.

"No. You don't get it. I like being a bounty hunter. I

like chasing bad guys and hunting down criminals. I don't want to do farm work. I hate those damn chickens with a passion."

Meg raised her eyes. "Ruby. Enough."

They'd had this argument several days ago, and Meg hadn't understood then, and apparently, she still didn't. Ruby wasn't giving up bounty hunting.

"Let's find out what's happened to Annabelle. Surely, she just got stuck in town, and she'll be home tomorrow morning."

"She hasn't been home for two days now. Something's wrong," Ruby said.

"Maybe she went to see Caroline. Maybe she needed some time away," Meg said, a worried tone in her voice.

Ruby shook her head. "That's not like her. She would have come home to tell us."

"You're right, Ruby," Zach replied. "It's not like Annabelle not to come home."

Meg sighed and glanced out the window of the farmhouse. "It's getting late, and we couldn't see a trail if we wanted to. Let's leave at first light and go into town. If we don't find Annabelle, we'll start searching for her right away."

Ruby nodded, knowing that had been her plan all along. She'd give Annabelle until the morning to get home, and then Ruby was out searching everywhere for her. "I'll get Caroline to watch the farm while we're gone."

"Hopefully, Annabelle's in town or with Caroline," Meg said, her tone sounding wistful.

Annabelle was the most logical, considerate one of the group. She would have contacted them, unless something had happened and she'd been unable to.

Maybe she was hurt or maybe…

God, her mind could go a thousand different directions and none of them good.

"She'd have let us know if she were staying with Caroline. She would have ridden back here and told us. Though she does deserve a few days away from this place. I can't imagine sitting here every day waiting for someone to arrive," Ruby said, trying to quiet her mind from all the scenarios that frightened her. She was worried. Annabelle was the homebody. The dependable sister.

"I'm sorry, Ruby. I'm very worried about Annabelle. It's just that I'm so happy right now, and I wanted the two of you to share our joy."

Ruby stood, walked over to Meg, and hugged her. "I'm happy for you, sis. I really am. And I know you're going to keep him in line."

Zach frowned at her. "Are you kidding me? I'm supposed to keep her from getting into trouble."

Ruby laughed, released Meg and then hugged Zach. "Welcome to the family, brother. Just let me warn you. You hurt my sister and I will fill you so full of lead you can't walk uphill."

Zach leaned back and smiled at Ruby. "Who's going to protect me from the likes of you girls? I think I'm the one that's in trouble here. Three women and one man. Would you get busy and find a husband, so I don't have to bear all the heat?"

She turned loose of his arms and stepped back. "You're going to fit in here real fine. I only hope nothing has happened to Annabelle."

"We'll find her in the morning," he promised.

*

Meg lay in the arms of her new husband in her parent's old bed. It felt awkward with a man once again in the house, but there hadn't been time for them to move her things to their new place. And she still felt apprehensive about her sisters.

The time had come for her to let them go and begin her own life, but it was harder than she'd expected, especially with Annabelle missing. What if something had happened to her sister?

"Do you think Annabelle's okay?" Meg asked her husband, enjoying the feel of his warm naked chest.

"I don't know. When I left the jail to find you, there was nothing going on in town that I knew of. No known wanted criminals roaming the area."

"Thanks for putting our plans on hold while we find Annabelle," she said, kissing his chest, letting her tongue slid around his nipple.

He rolled her onto her back and slid his body down hers. She loved the feel of him on top of her, skin to skin, chest to chest, abdomen to… Oh God, she loved the feel of her big, strong man.

"We'll find her tomorrow. She'll be fine; you'll see. We'll give her the news, and then we'll be able to set up our home."

She sighed as warmth, mingled with love, crested in her chest to overflowing. "Our home. I love that sound. "

He chuckled. "I love what you're doing to me."

Meg batted her eyelashes at him, like she'd seen Ruby do to countless men. "Whatever am I doing to you?"

He growled deep and low in his throat. "You know exactly what you're doing. And it's working."

She giggled. "Well then, cowboy, I guess you better

get busy."

"With pleasure, love."

*

Annabelle had never been more miserable in her life. The sky had opened up, drenching them with a cold, wet rain that felt like arrows piercing her skin in the strong wind. Water dripped from her clothing, her skin, her eyelids, even her nose, and the weather showed no signs of letting up anytime soon. Lightning flashed like daggers being thrown from the sky, and thunder clapped like a stampede of cattle. And yet they rode on. Slower due to the slippery rocks and the sucking mud.

"We're close," Beau called back to her.

She didn't say anything and he turned to gaze at her. She gave him a thumbs-up signal, as her teeth chattered from the cold.

"You okay?" he asked.

"Yessss," she said, her teeth clicking together, her lips numb.

He shook his head, and ten minutes later, she saw an opening in the side of the hill—a small cavity with bushes surrounding the entryway that would only accommodate them, not their horses—a cave with bats. Small, creepy, stinking, pooping, lice-ridden bats that made her skin shudder worse than the chills she was feeling at this moment.

A warm fire and a place out of the wind and rain would feel great right now, and she'd pick the cave over the elements, but that didn't mean she had to like bats. No, sir, she would tolerate them, but that was all.

When they halted their horses, Beau came over and helped her alight. They were both sodden to the skin, and her skirts made dismounting difficult. "What happened to the farmhouse you were going to drop me at?"

"Haven't seen one. I thought for sure there would be one before now. Guess, you'll just have to stay the night again."

She frowned at him. "I'm not going in that cave alone. You go first."

A grin spread across his face. "You were all tough before. What happened?"

"I let the weaker and dumber go first."

He shook his head. "Thanks. I'll remember that."

"It's raining out here. Do you think we could possibly get out of the cold before we get struck by lightning?"

As if to concur with her, a big clap of thunder rumbled through the valley.

"Maybe so," he said and led the way into the rock shelter. "Watch for snakes or wolves or mountain lions."

"Oh, that's comforting." She stood behind him, thinking if there were anything in there, they would eat him first. By the time they got around to her, she'd be halfway back to Zenith.

"Look someone left firewood. We can start a fire."

"Good, I'm freezing."

He took another step into the darkness and glanced around. "Anybody in here?"

"Oh, I'm sure a big old mountain lion is going to answer you back and say *no, I've left town.*"

He laughed. "Maybe not, but if he were in there, I bet I'd hear a growl or rumble or something to warn me away. I'd rather know now before I get a fire built and we get all cozy."

"True," she said, peering into the darkness, wishing she could see past the entranceway.

"I think we're good," he said.

Annabelle began to relax, but she wouldn't let her guard down until they had a fire blazing big enough to warn predators away and warm her. She turned and gazed out across the valley. They were a little ways up the side of the mountain, but not so high their horses would be far away.

"Let's get that fire started."

"What about bats?" she asked.

"Will you quit worrying about the damn bats? There might not be any in here."

"Maybe not, but until I know for certain, I'm going to be on the lookout." The fear of bats flying into her hair was a terrifying thought. She cringed at the image that filled her mind.

Beau walked around the perimeter and then knelt beside the wood. Strategically, he built a fire close to the entrance, so the smoke would billow out, but back far enough no one could see the flames from outside.

"Boy, did we get lucky. They even left some fire starter to get the blaze going," he said, stacking the kindling together.

She watched him, noticing that even he shivered.

"Do you have any other clothes with you," he asked, not looking at her as he struck the flint to the sticks.

Oh, she didn't like his train of thought. She knew without thinking what he was going to suggest and it would be a definite, no.

"I'm fine."

"God, woman, I took you for being smarter than that. You are not fine. You are shivering so hard you're shaking water all over the cavern. Start shucking those wet clothes."

That was not going to happen. Being naked in front of a man, any man, but especially one she'd only known less than forty-eight hours was impossible. Sure, she was shivering like a lizard looking for a hot rock, but she'd manage.

She glowered at him. "I'm not removing my clothes in the presence of a man I've known for only forty-eight hours. A criminal, a bank—"

"Yeah, yeah, I know. I know I'm the spawn of Satan, who is not going to let you catch your death of pneumonia. You can put on my extra set of clothes, and I'll go around naked."

"You most certainly will not." The idea of him walking around without any clothes, his man parts exposed, was intriguing, but not enough to keep her inside the cave.

"Well, I'm not stupid enough to get deathly sick from wet clothes. I'd rather sit here bare naked in all my glory in front of a fire than be wet and cold."

"But…"

"Honey, I'm a man. Clothes are not all that important."

Yes, but his strong shoulders and well-defined thighs, his flat abdomen and his well built chest were not what she wanted to stare at all night long.

"Maybe to you they're not."

"You're so right." He stood from the blazing fire. "Dang, I hate to leave this fire, but I need to unsaddle our horses."

"I'll help you."

Staying alone in this cave was not really something she felt comfortable with. Even being out in the elements with an outlaw was better than staying by herself in a rock cavern where animals lived. *Bats*.

"No, you can have the privacy of the cave to disrobe. Now get to it."

"And if I don't?"

He turned and stared at her, his emerald eyes dancing with shiny delight. A grin turned up the corners of his mouth. "I've never had the pleasure of forcing a woman to undress for me. It might be kind of fun. I'm game if you are?"

She wrinkled her nose and mouth at him. The man was a huge pain, and while she didn't want to shed her clothes, the thought of him undressing her was even worse.

"You better get started, unless you want me to help you along."

He walked out of the cavern and she took a moment to glance around. If she stepped out of the glow of the fire, it would very quickly become dark. Very dark.

A squeaking noise came from the back of the cavern.

Peering into the darkness, she tried to locate the noise. Something buzzed her head, and she realized bats were flying straight toward her. Screaming, she turned and ran out of the cavern, shooing the creepy mammals away from her hair.

She ran smack dab into Beau. He wrapped his big, strong arms around her and held her, tremors rumbling through him though he never chuckled out loud. "You're okay. I'm sorry. It's about the time of day when the bats leave the cave to go hunting. I should have warned you."

Doubling up her fists, she hit him smack in the chest. "You knew I didn't like bats. You knew I was afraid."

His hands rubbed her back in a soothing way that calmed her. "Sugar, you're the fiercest woman I've ever met, and I never thought a few bats would send you running for cover."

"If I'd had my pistol, they'd all be dead."

Her petticoat pistol was still attached beneath her skirt, but she would have had to stop running to reach the weapon. There was no way she was staying in that cavern, while they swarmed out of the opening.

"If you'd shot at the damn bats, there would have been bullets ricocheting off the walls of the cave."

"Oh." She was quiet for a moment and still in his arms. Heat from his body began to seep into her, and she stopped shaking from the cold. "I don't like bats."

"I know," he said, his voice soft and low, close to her ear. Warmth trickled through her like honey, seeping into her bones and crevices. Into places, she'd never considered getting hot. A sense of safety and security filled her. She liked being in his arms.

Oh no. No, no, no.

She pushed out of his embrace. "Thanks for the warning."

"What warning?" he asked, smiling at her.

"My point exactly."

With a lot of trepidation, she walked back into the cave. She didn't see any more of the flying mammals and hoped they had now vacated the area for the night. But they would return just as the sun crept over the edge of the earth. Maybe she and Beau would be gone by then.

Revulsion swept through her as she imaged them, their eyes glowing in the darkness. A shiver ran down her spine.

Beau walked back into the hideout, carrying his saddle. "See, they're gone for the night."

She glared at him but didn't respond. She watched as

he opened his saddlebags and pulled out an extra shirt.

"Here, you can wear this, and I'll take the pants."

"What if I want the shirt *and* the pants?"

He grinned at her. "Fine by me. I don't mind sitting around a campfire naked. I might even be warmer that way."

"You'd do so just to annoy me, too."

Reaching out, he clucked her beneath the chin. "Get changed. You're back to shivering. I'll see if I can string a rope close to the fire where the clothes can dry."

How could she argue with him when she knew what he was telling her was the truth, and she was miserable in her heavy wet skirt that was collecting mud on the hem. Soon she'd have her own farm right on the bottom of her skirt.

"Stay outside, while I change."

A big clap of thunder made the ground shudder beneath her.

"Sure, I'd love to stand outside in the pouring rain, so you can maintain your privacy."

Her pistol was still strapped beneath her skirt, and she needed to remove it without him seeing her little Baby Dragoon. She wanted to keep that gun close. So far, she hadn't felt the need to use it on him, but when the time came, she wanted her trusty gun within reach. Near enough to surprise him.

Hopefully, her sisters were already looking for her, and when they found her, she'd help bring him to justice.

Quickly, she pulled the water laden skirt off her body along with her petticoat. When she rode her horse, she only wore one of the lacey undergarments because they were too bulksome and puffed up way too much on the saddle. She always had Meg make her skirts with enough width so she could spread them over her horse's back. And now she was paying the price for that extra material.

"Are you dressed?"

"Stay out," she replied and hurriedly undid the buttons on her blouse. With a yank, she removed the sodden outer shirt. Even her chemise was soaked clear to her skin, and she could see the puckered outline of her nipples through the material.

Nothing was hidden from view through the clingy, wet material. While he was still outside, she slipped on his shirt and buttoned it all the way up to the top. The shirt tails hung down past her hips, but still she left her pantaloons on. They were wet, but they'd dry, especially with her standing next to the fire.

When he came back into the cave, she had pulled his bedroll out and laid it on the ground next to the fire. Her clothes were draped over a rock since she didn't want them to lie in the dirt.

His emerald eyes glided over her, turning a dark green that smoldered. "You look pretty darn cute in that outfit, but I'd lose the pantaloons. They're getting the shirt wet."

"I didn't ask for your opinion." Like hell, she was going to shed the pantaloons. That would leave her naked from the waist down. And while his shirt hung down below her buttocks, she didn't like the vulnerability of being exposed.

His brows rose and he shook his head. "You'll be naked if that shirt gets too wet."

"Do you just like to say that word? Does it give you a thrill?"

He tilted his head and thought about it for a moment. "Yeah, I think it does."

Darn it! He was a bigger pain than her sister Meg had been while growing up. "I'm not going unclothed."

"Suit yourself."

He strung a rope across the cave, close enough to the fire so that the clothes would dry, but not burn. Then he put another log on the blaze and began to unbutton his shirt.

"Excuse me," she said when he started to unbutton his pants.

Glancing at her, he shrugged his shoulders. "What?"

"Can't you change somewhere else?"

"Sure, I'll step into the bedroom and close the door."

"Smartass."

"Yes, I am," he admitted. "Close your eyes, if you don't want to look."

But that was the problem. She did want to see. She wanted to see the hard planes she had felt beneath his shirt. She wanted a glance at the firm buttocks and thighs she'd seen riding a horse, she wanted to see...

A rush of heat thrummed through her blood, causing her breath to quicken at the thought of him naked before her.

No, no, no, no. He was not the kind of man, she wanted in her life. He was not an appropriate suitor.

But he was still mighty fine looking.

She closed her eyes tightly and he laughed. Then she opened them just a peek to watch as he stripped off his pants. He turned his back to her and removed his long johns, giving her a brief glimpse of his strong muscled back, his firm butt cheeks and thighs that would garner any woman's attention.

Her pulse raced at the sight of his firm butt and part of her wanted him to turn around. She bit her lip, trying to refrain from groaning at the sight. She just wanted a glimpse at what he looked like.

He slipped on his dry, clean pants and turned to face her, his chest naked. *Wow, wow, wow* was all she could think when she stared at him. A shiver passed through her, and it wasn't the cold.

Quickly, she hung her clothes on the line to dry, making sure her gun and the money she'd hidden inside the folds of her petticoat were hidden where they couldn't be seen. There were some things he didn't need to know.

She walked over to the fire and got as close to the blaze as she could get, hoping the heat would dry her pantaloons.

Warmth caressed the back of her legs, and she didn't look at Beau. She didn't want to gaze at his half-naked body and think about how she'd just like to run her hand down his smooth muscled skin—trail her finger down his shoulder, his back, his buttocks.

She heard him walk over to the clothesline and hang his pants, long johns, and shirt to dry.

"Do we have any rations left?" she asked.

"Of course, we do. I come prepared, unlike some people I know."

She sighed. He was right. She'd not been as prepared for this trip as she should have been. But she'd left on a whim, though she'd never admit that to him. And now that impulse was a problem.

"We were supposed to already be back in town by now."

"And how did that work out for you?"

"Shut up, Beau."

He chuckled.

Her pantaloons were starting to feel very warm. The scent of something burning reached her nose, and then suddenly, Beau was throwing her onto the bedroll, beating her legs.

"Gosh, damn it, woman, you are a pain in the ass."

"Get off me."

"Your underwear was on fire."

With him still on top of her, she glanced down at the bottom of her pantaloons. The lace around the edge had burned off but hadn't reached her skin.

Her heart skipped a beat at the thought of her clothes catching fire. Yet, he was lying on top of her, and she was beginning to feel a different kind of warmth. She could feel his bare chest and the thump of his heart against her. They landed on the bedroll, but now he was half-on and half-off of her. He was gazing at her, his eyes dark and burning with some emotion she didn't recognize. A heat that had nothing to do with her pantaloons catching fire suddenly engulfed her.

His half-naked body was touching her, with only his shirt separating their chests. Her breathing sounded loud and rushed in the cave with only a crack and pop of the fire.

"How can one woman get into so much trouble and yet look so innocent and beautiful? How can you be so tempting and sweet and luscious one moment and the next I'm ready to kill you? And how can I go another minute, looking at those full lips without tasting them? Damn it, I don't want to do this, but I've got to," he said, his voice husky, sending shivers of anticipation through her.

He was going to kiss her. She watched as his mouth lowered to hers, and she realized she wanted his kiss.

His mouth moved over hers, tempting and teasing and tasting of her like she'd never been kissed before. And she never had.

This was her first kiss and whatever expectations she'd had were quickly dispelled. It was much better than she'd imagined. His hands gripped her face, holding her hostage to his lips, holding her immobile as he took her lips between his own. Savagely, he slanted his mouth over hers as his tongue persuaded her to open. He tasted her thoroughly, completely, and so convincingly her heart was ready to explode in her chest.

Hot, heavy, hunger filled her as his mouth took her like the storm that raged outside. Wild, consuming, and awakening feelings she'd never experienced before. She arched her back, needing more, wanting more of the passion this man had awakened inside her.

Her flesh was on fire with the need for this man. She wanted to remove the barriers between them. Running her fingers down his silken, muscled shoulders, she wanted to touch him everywhere, feel his skin, taste him.

God, she didn't know what it was she wanted, but she wanted this to continue. She didn't want this to stop. She wanted...

A shot rang out in the night, not far from their cave.

Beau bolted into a sitting position. He jumped up ran to the entrance, and peered into the darkness. Another shot sounded and he grabbed his wet shirt and ran outside in the rain, with his guns drawn, leaving Annabelle alone, panting in a bat cave.

Chapter Four

Beau didn't come back to the cave until late last night. He'd been unable to locate the source of the gunshots, and yet, it wasn't the danger outside that had kept him searching. More the danger inside the cavern. Kissing Annabelle had been one of the stupidest moves he'd made this trip. That woman's lips were sweeter than anything he'd ever experienced. And being a lonely man on the trail with a sweet, seductive woman was not conducive to staying alive.

His focus had to remain on reaching Fort Worth. Sometime today, he had to locate a farmhouse and rid himself of this luscious, appealing, provocative woman. Annabelle's full breasts and curvaceous hips were enough to tempt even a sin-buster to stray. Enough to tempt Beau into acting on urges that had his imagination envisioning how beautiful her naked skin would look in the moonlight. Wondering if her skin was as silky to the touch as he imagined.

Once again, he'd slept on the ground, not trusting himself to come near her in his bedroll. She'd been alone, though all he'd wanted to do was crawl inside those blankets and finish what he'd started. Now, this morning, she slept on, while he packed the saddlebags.

She stirred and sleepily said, "We need to leave before the bats return."

"They came back almost an hour ago."

She sat straight up in the bedroll, her hair tousled, and rubbed her eyes.

God, she was an alluring woman who had his *attention* rising to full mast.

"Why didn't you wake me?"

"And listen to you screaming and running out of the cavern again? No, thank you. Not the way I wanted to start my morning." Oh no, if she'd become upset, he'd have been tempted to calm her, and that would have involved touching her, holding her, kissing her, and then they would never have come out of this cave all day.

She scrunched up her face at him in a frown. "Ha-ha!"

"Keep making that face and the bats may think you're one of them." He had to get them back on the lighthearted side and give his tortured manhood a rest.

"You are certainly full of vinegar this morning. What were those shots you went chasing after?"

"Nothing. Absolutely nothing." Whatever gunshots he'd heard echoing in the dark had not been close enough for him to find.

Rising, she wrapped the blanket around her waist and walked to the opening. She gazed out at the valley below them, the sun just now peeking over the eastern horizon. "It looks so beautiful and peaceful."

"And yet, it's on the edge of some of the most ruthless territories in Texas."

"I tried to stay awake and wait on you, but I couldn't keep my eyes open."

"That's okay. It was late when I got back." This woman was trouble, and he needed to put as much distance between the two of them as possible.

He walked to where she was standing. "We need to find a farmhouse today, where I can leave you."

She turned toward him, her blue eyes shadowed with surprise. "You're going to leave me behind after we shared that kiss last night."

"Because of that kiss last night," he said. "I'm running for my life, and I don't need to endanger you."

She stared at him, her eyes swimming with tears. "Have you considered not being an outlaw? If you work at it, you can be a good guy. I bet if you talked to the sheriff, there could be some way you could repay your crimes and obey the law."

A laugh escaped before he could hold back his response. "Sugar, my crimes are bad enough the only thing waiting for me when the law catches me is a short rope on a tall tree."

Annabelle McKenzie was still a woman, and he'd seen the glitter in her eyes this morning. That kiss had affected her just as much as him, and he needed to dispel any notions she was cooking up in that female brain of hers of the two of them together, sharing forever. The next sodbuster he came across, he was leaving her behind.

"Now quit stalling. We need to get going."

A frown flitted across her face, and her sapphire eyes darkened, her lips tightening.

"I guess then we better go if we're going to find that farmhouse," she said, her voice cold. "I'm sure my sisters won't be far behind. Then we'll catch you and collect our five hundred dollar reward."

Her sisters…sometimes he wondered if they were a figment of her imagination. Women bounty hunters? Really?

"Oh sugar, I should be worth more than that. You need to ask for a thousand," he said, glad to see they were back to baiting each other. At least this way, he wasn't thinking about how he wanted to slant his lips over her smart, sassy mouth until she clung to him.

Yet, there was still a part of him that was sad to see the way she'd tensed at the realization he would hang if the law caught him.

She strode over to where her skirt had hung all night to dry. "Why don't you step outside and I'll get dressed."

"You sure you don't need my help," he said, trying to goad her temper. If she hated him, then he wouldn't need to worry about her wanting his kisses. Though, his body was hard with wanting her.

"Get out of here. I'm quite capable of dressing myself. I'll hand you your shirt once I'm dressed." She turned her back to him, clearly dismissing him.

Women had more thorns than prickly cactus. Hers was one damn fine kiss, but nothing had changed. She wanted to collect the bounty being offered on him, and he had to get to Fort Worth.

"Just say the word and I'll be your lady's maid."

"Not if you want to live."

Walking out of the cave into the morning light, he chuckled to himself. Riling her up had chased away the stars he'd seen shining in her eyes.

Now, staring out across the valley, he breathed deeply and realized he smelled smoke, and it wasn't from their campfire. Somewhere down in this valley, there must be a farm, and some farmer was burning wood. The perfect place to leave her behind. He needed to find that sodbuster and drop her off soon. Very soon. Before his traitorous lips tasted more of Annabelle's luscious mouth. Before he ripped off her pantaloons and experienced her sweet womanly body.

*

Beau turned his horse down the lane. Smoke spiraled high above the trees, and an eerie silence had him glancing behind every scrub brush. Uneasiness twirled along his spine as he realized the birds no longer squawked. Stillness hung over the area, and the smoke seemed heavier with a pungent odor that didn't smell like brush.

Something wasn't right and he didn't know what, yet.

Annabelle rode beside him. She'd been quieter than normal this morning. Almost as if she'd withdrawn from him and didn't want to engage anymore. Like she was pushing him away from her, she'd been colder than a bartender at quitting time.

This was the very reason a man a like him shouldn't be kissing a woman like Annabelle. Though she wasn't a prim and proper, Bible thumping, miss, she wasn't a saloon girl waiting on a client either. And if he had the time, he would have liked to have gotten to know her better, but now, he was going to leave her behind and trust she found her way back home.

"Oh, God," she said and pulled her horse to a stop.

Two bodies lay on the ground, not far from each other. Smoke drifted from the burned out skeleton of the house. Only the smoking, scarred walls of the home still stood.

Beau held his breath, alert, searching the area for danger. His eyes scanned the bushes and trees around the house, his palm resting on his gun. "Stay here."

"Like hell," she said.

And together the two of them rode slowly into the yard of the house.

"Do you think it was Indians?"

"No," he said, knowing there hadn't been an Indian attack in this area for years. This looked more like the work of the Harris gang.

He threw his leg over his saddle and slide off his horse. He hoped she'd stay put, but she stepped down off her horse. Taking the reins of both animals, she led them into the yard of the burned out home, while he approached with his gun drawn.

"Stay with the horses," he demanded

She didn't respond. He went over to the first body and checked for a pulse. The young man's body was cold. He had a bullet wound to his chest. He'd died quickly.

He walked over to the second body, an older gentleman, and rolled him over. The man gasped and his eyes opened, surprising Beau that he still lived. The old man's pupils were large and dark, and Beau could see he was in pain.

"My son?" he asked.

"He's dead."

The man closed his eyes, squeezing them together to keep the tears from falling.

"Where are you hurt? Who else lived here?"

The old man shook his head. "No need. It was just me and my boy. They took our horses and scattered our livestock."

"Who? Tell me what happened."

The man licked his lips. "There were five riders.

They called the leader, William."

The Harris gang.

Annabelle stepped up beside Beau with a dipper of water for the man.

"Here," she said as she lifted his blood soaked shirt, locating his bullet wound in his side. She shook her head, indicating the wound was fatal.

Beau lifted the man gingerly, so he could sip the water.

"When did they attack?" Beau asked.

Finishing the water, the man sighed. "The bastards had dinner with us and then attacked late last night. They wanted our horses. I refused to hand them over. They jumped up. Shot Charlie first and then me."

The shots Beau had heard were the Harris gang attacking this settler and his son.

The old man's hand clutched at Beau's shirt. "Please, bury us next to my wife." He coughed and blood poured from his mouth. His eyes drifted closed, and with one last gasp, his head dropped onto his chest.

"Damn it!" Beau said as he laid the man's head down.

He stood and strode away, running his hands through his hair. This man and his son were only trying to make a living, working their farm. Because the Harris gang came across them, they were now both dead.

He kicked a rock with his boot, sending it flying. *Damn.* He should have been here. Maybe he could have stopped them from killing this innocent man and his son.

"He's at peace," she said quietly. Then she stood and walked a short distance away.

She stared out at the wilderness, and he could tell she was watching the area. He was grateful, as it gave him time to control his anger at this man's senseless death.

She strolled around the yard and stopped at a door that was angled out of the ground. She lifted the entrance and descended the steps.

Damn it. He didn't need her to get hurt. He rushed over to where she'd disappeared into a root cellar. Hurriedly, he followed her into the underground storage that was filled with homemade canned goods. "Come on. We need to get going."

"No. Look. The man has tools. We can bury him and his son."

Beau could fulfill the old man's wish if they could find his wife's grave.

There were also canned goods and potatoes. "Collect what food items you think we can carry, and I'll get started looking for the family plot. We need to get out of here as quickly as possible."

"We?"

He turned and stared at her and released a heavy sigh. If the Harris gang were attacking small farms, she wouldn't be any safer with a farmer than she would be with him. At least together, they had a better chance of survival than leaving her with a man who wasn't quite as quick on the draw and wouldn't recognize trouble when he saw it coming through his gate.

A man just like this farmer.

"I'm not leaving you behind at an empty farmhouse," he said, staring into her gaze, wanting to get lost there—to let her ease the sorrow he felt at this man's useless death.

"Good. I would have followed you. I'm collecting that bounty."

He shook his head. "You're going to be disappointed,

woman."

"No, I'm not." She dumped an armful of canned goods into his hands. "You can carry these up the stairs."

"Yes, ma'am," he said, sarcastically. "I'm certainly glad the Harris gang didn't find these. We won't be going hungry for a while." He climbed the wooden steps to the outside world and unloaded the glass jars on the where Annabelle could find them, then turned and went back down.

At least with him, he could protect her until he could get her to Fort Worth. But right now, she was looking at him like he was a cold, hostile beast. If she had a weapon, she'd have used it on him. And maybe, just maybe, with the thoughts that had run through his head about the things he'd like to do to her, she was justified in feeling that way.

He watched her as she collected some bacon, potatoes, and beans from the root cellar.

"I don't think we have room for anything else," she said. "Shame they didn't leave a bedroll down here."

"Yeah," he said, thinking of how hard that ground was every night and how tempting it had been to curl up beside her last night and share her body heat. Only problem was his body wanted to share other parts of her womanly flesh.

He crawled up the stairs with a shovel in hand and helped her up with his other hand. "Now, let's find his wife's grave. I'd like to bury them before we leave."

*

An hour later, Annabelle helped Beau drag the bodies of the dead man and his son over to the newly dug hole. She shuddered as they rolled the bodies into the empty grave. A gruesome task, but they'd fulfilled their promise to the dying man. And while she was glad, she never wanted to have to do something so horrible again.

Beau stood and wiped the sweat from his brow. Even though it was springtime, the sun had beat down mercilessly on them, while he'd dug out a shallow grave for both bodies.

When he'd announced he would be leaving her at the first farm they came to, she'd been mad enough to eat the Devil with his horns on. Hadn't that kiss affected him the way it had her? She'd been ready to yank off his clothes and surrender like a willow in the wind.

And then this morning, he'd fried the dew off her first kiss when he'd acted like nothing had changed. *Nothing.* That kiss meant nothing to him. Like she meant nothing and when he'd told her the law had a rope with his name on it, she'd known there was no sense in getting all excited by Beau Samuel's kisses.

There were five hundred dollars attached to his name, and she aimed to garner that money with or without her sisters' help. She'd turn this bastard in and then return home to think about his kisses, while taking her pistol out for target practice. There was a tin can with his face on it waiting back home.

After they dropped the bodies inside the graves, they stepped back and caught their breaths. Sweat trickled down Beau's face, and the muscles of his arms looked large and beefy. A strong muscular man, Beau Samuel was not someone you messed with.

"It's warm today," he said, taking his handkerchief and swiping the beaded moisture from his brow.

His tongue wet his lips, and she had the urge to step into his arms and experience the pleasure of his mouth once more. Just the memory of his lips on hers had her

67

body heating from the inside out. But kissing him again wasn't going to happen. He was an outlaw, and she didn't need that kind of heartache. She just needed the five hundred dollars reward money.

"Yeah, it is," she said, gazing at him in the sunshine. There was something deliciously incongruent about him.

How many outlaws would have taken the time to fulfill the wishes of a dying man by burying his body and his son's by his dead wife? And how many outlaws would have stopped after kissing her last night?

Was there really honor among thieves or was Beau Samuel different?

"Bow your head and let's say a little prayer," he said, looking at her with a sheepish look on his face, like he was afraid she'd say something about him praying over the dead man and his son.

"Father, accept these souls into your loving arms and forgive them for any sins they may have committed. In your son's name, amen."

Annabelle raised her head and didn't say a word. An outlaw saying a prayer over the men his gang had killed? She shook her head. This man was very complex, but he was still an outlaw with a bounty on his head, which she intended to collect.

"As soon as I finish covering the bodies, we need to get on the trail. We've already been here longer than we should have been."

"You don't think they'll come back, do you?"

"No, but I'm not sticking around to find out. We need to get further down the trail before dark."

"Why are they searching for you?" she asked.

He took his canteen and lifted it over his head, letting the water splash down over his face. Then he wiped the extra moisture away with his handkerchief.

As he cleared the water droplets from his face, his gaze lingered on her. "I'm a member of the gang. After the hold-up in Wichita, I hid the bank money. They want their share."

A small piece of her heart hardened at the realization he was not a good guy. Whatever doubts she'd had about whether or not he was truly a wanted man and outlaw disappeared. The man had robbed a bank then hidden the money from the rest of the gang. No wonder there were five men chasing him. No wonder they wanted to kill him.

"Do you want a share of the money?" he asked, with a teasing grin on his face.

A part of her wanted to slap that silly smile right off his face. Farmers and ranchers had worked hard for that cash only to have it stolen. And he was acting like it was nothing. She took a deep breath and built a wall around her heart against this man. She smiled. "Not on your life. What I want is the bounty on your head and I aim to get it."

She turned and walked away from him, letting him stew on her goal. He may have thought she'd given up, but she hadn't. And actually, she had him to thank for that. Because if he hadn't given her that kiss last night, she might have returned home and sent her sister Ruby after him.

But now it was personal. That kiss and his consequent rejection this morning had sealed her resolve to hand him over to the law. She wanted the first man who had ever kissed her to rot in jail, and she planned on helping him find his way there.

*

Back on the trail, the easy banter between them from yesterday had disappeared. There was a tense silence, and Annabelle knew they were both thinking about that poor farmer and his son. The Harris gang included some of the worst outlaws she'd ever heard of, not the usual longriders Meg and Ruby pursued. Silently, she prayed her sisters were on their way. They were almost two days ride from Zenith, and with any luck, her sisters had seen her tracks and would find her.

Every time they stopped, she'd left her initials in the dirt or a scrap of her petticoat when Beau wasn't looking, trusting her sisters would find the signs and know they were on the right trail.

Annabelle raised up in the saddle, trying to give her bones a rest from the constant jarring.

"Saddle weary?" Beau asked.

"A little," she said.

"You know, you haven't slowed me down much. I'm surprised. You must do a lot of work around your farm," he said, glancing over at her with admiration.

"Since I'm there most of the time by myself, I don't have much choice," she responded.

"I thought you had two sisters."

"They're out bounty hunting, so we can keep the farm."

He shook his head and laughed. "Oh, yes, the bounty hunter sisters. I'm not certain I believe they're real. Kind of like that husband and sheriff you mentioned the other night."

Maybe he had a small point about her husband and sheriff. But she couldn't wait to see her sisters again. "When you meet them, you'll know it's real."

"I grew up on a farm," he said.

"Really?" she said, unable to imagine him working in the fields. "What made you decide to leave?"

"We lost the farm and had to move into town."

A frown furrowed his brow, and she could see the memory wasn't a good one, but she couldn't feel sorry for this man. She had to keep her barriers up between them.

They rode along the trail, meandering around some tall scrub oak. She glanced over and saw a small lane. At the end of that wide trail, a house sat. She could see smoke spiraling from the chimney. "Hey, there's a farmhouse. "

Part of her was ready to get off the trail and the other part of her didn't want to leave him. Both parts knew it was best if they separated from Beau. There was a powerful attraction between them, and it could only lead to heartache.

He glanced over at it and nodded his head. "Yeah, I saw it a ways back."

"Aren't we going to stop?" she asked.

"Nope."

"What do you mean nope? You couldn't wait to get rid of me yesterday."

"I've changed my mind."

"Oh, no." She pulled her horse to a stop as hot white anger rushed through her blood, shocking her. "I'm not going any further. First, you told me you would tie me up and leave me on the trail. Then you told me at the first farmhouse we came to you would leave me, and now, you're saying nope. Well, I'm the one who's putting an end to this little adventure we're on. I'm done. I'm calling it quits."

He glanced over at her, a daring glint in his emerald

gaze. "What happened to getting your five hundred dollar bounty?"

Like a teakettle, the pressure was mounting, and she was about ready to explode. "I'm still going to get it. But I'm going to wait until my sisters catch up to me, and then we'll go after you together."

A smile graced his face. "That's my smart, sassy mouth girl. I knew you wouldn't give up on getting that reward."

"Hell no, that reward will make the farm ours."

"I'm real happy for you. But I'm not going to leave you with strangers at a farmhouse that might be attacked by the Harris gang. I'm not having your dead body on my conscience."

Aargh. She wanted to leave him behind. She wanted to get away from his boyish charm and his sweet, tempting mouth and his hard chest. She wanted to find her sisters and then come after him with a vengeance. But the thought of dying like that farmer and his son was terrifying.

"And that's better than being attacked on the trail in your company? Don't you think they'll kill you and me both if we're found together?"

"Maybe. But you saw what they did to that farmer. Is that what you want? Do you want to take a chance? I can protect you better than a sodbuster."

Annabelle's emotions felt like a broomtail flippin in the wind in a cornfield, blown in every direction. Part of her longed to stay with the farmer, part of her wanted her sisters to find them on the trail, and part of her wanted to stay with Beau and for his lips to explore hers once again. "I want my sisters to catch up and help me wrangle you to the nearest sheriff."

He grinned at her. "I can't wait to meet these sisters of yours."

"You may regret saying that."

"Come on, let's go. You're going with me."

Why now and why with this man had she suddenly experienced her first kiss? Why an outlaw, a man her papa would have hauled into town for his bounty? And why like this out on the prairie?

Because of her own silly pride for thinking her sisters had all the fun, while she sat at home and talked to the chickens.

Chapter Five

Later that afternoon, Beau's worst nightmare came true. He glanced behind him and saw the Harris gang riding hard toward them, sending his heart to pounding and his breath straining. He had a choice. Try to get away from them with Annabelle, or stop and act like he was glad to see the gang he belonged to and he'd been busy searching for the outlaws everywhere.

Though he hated the second option, he couldn't help but think it would serve him better than trying to outrun them and risking either himself or Annabelle being shot.

He pulled his horse to a halt and glanced over at Annabelle. "Listen," he said, his voice stern. "The Harris gang is about a half mile behind us. Follow my lead and don't do anything stupid. You're my wife. Do you hear me? Don't disagree or you'll be servicing five randy cowboys. Are we clear?"

Her blue eyes widened with fear, as she pulled up next to his horse. "You better get me out of this alive, or I will haunt you in hell. Do you understand me?"

He reached out and ran his fingertips across the smooth skin of her face. "Sugar, just be your usual charming self."

The sound of horse's hooves brought his attention back to the situation at hand. Beau waved to the riders like he was happy to see them and said a quick prayer that they would not be dead before sunset.

The riders surrounded them, with William coming up beside Beau. "Where in the hell have you been?"

"What do you mean? I told you when we split up I would hide the bank robbery money, and I'd catch up to you on the way to Fort Worth." God, he hoped they believed that lie. Or else any second now he'd be feeling a bullet entering his brain.

"I've spent the last three days looking for you," William said, his dark eyes glowing with hatred. "I've half a mind to shoot you right now."

Beau shrugged his shoulders, pretending it didn't matter, while remembering the man William had shot and left for dead on the trail. "If you don't ever want to see that bank money again, that's your choice."

Silence filled the air as William stared at Beau, his eyes searching Beau's face.

"Once I lost that posse, I hid the money. Then I was passing by Zenith, and I stopped and married my childhood sweetheart. Gentlemen, meet my lovely wife, Annabelle."

Maybe since he'd brought his wife, they'd believe he wasn't trying to steal the money away from them. Though, in a sense, he did plan on keeping the cash from them.

The men whistled, but William didn't look convinced. He shook his head. "Why in the hell did you bring your wife out on the trail?"

"Now, I know what you're thinking, William, but it's not true. I wouldn't have brought Annabelle if I was trying steal the hold-up money. My plan was to get the money, find you, and put Annabelle at Crockett, where your family is waiting for you. That way she'd be safe, while we're out earning a living."

William growled like a ravenous beast. "Where did you hide the money?"

"We're two days' ride away," Beau said, trying to act surprised at the outlaw's reaction. "It's near the Red River. Right on the way to visit your wife and family."

"I should kill you right here for disappearing with the money."

Beau expected to see the flash of the gun's nozzle any second. William hadn't hesitated when he'd killed that poor man for being drunk. The only thing working in Beau's favor was the missing money, or he knew he would have been dead by now.

He shrugged like his life meant nothing, while he held his breath. "That's your choice, but with that posse breathing down our neck, I didn't want to take a chance of getting caught and all of us losing the money and hanging from a tree."

Refusing to back down, Beau stared at William. The man was a killer. A murderer of innocents, and evil men seemed to flock to him. Did malevolence attract more evil?

"You'll take us to the money tomorrow. Then we'll take your wife to join the other women," William said, though his voice was cold.

They had until Beau located the money, and then he felt certain William would put a bullet in their brains. Sometime between now and the time they reached the Red River, he had to get Annabelle and himself out of this man's clutches. "Sounds like a plan."

William signaled to his men, and they all fell into line. Beau glanced over at Annabelle, who hadn't said a word during all this time.

She pulled her horse alongside Beau, and they rode side by side with the Harris gang surrounding them. Oh no, they weren't letting Beau out of their sights again.

"What did you say your wife's name was Samuel?" William asked.

"Annabelle."

Beau held his breath, fear stealing over him like a bad drunk. If she didn't answer William's questions to his liking, the grass could soon be waving over them.

"You never mentioned no childhood sweetheart," William said, gazing at Annabelle suspiciously.

"Well, I hadn't exactly planned on marrying her right away," Beau admitted, his nerves stretching taut as William stared at Annabelle.

"How's married life treating you, Mrs. Samuel?"

Annabelle huffed out an exasperated breath.

Oh dear, he knew this was going to be good before she even opened her mouth.

"How do you think? This is supposed to be our honeymoon, and so far all we've done is search for you guys. I'm ready for us to settle down, spend some time together, and begin a family. Hell, I didn't even get a proper wedding night." She sighed, and her eyes looked dreamily at Beau.

God, the woman was incorrigible. She was telling a bunch of outlaws she wanted the two of them to start working on getting her pregnant. What the hell was she thinking?

William chuckled. "Why did you marry Beau so quickly?"

A smirk filled her beautiful full lips, and her sapphire eyes twinkled. "Well, my pa caught us kissing in the barn, and the next thing I knew we were standing before a preacher."

"You got caught, Beau," William said with a smile. "It happens to the best of us."

"That's why I've been missing. It was get married or be put to bed with a pick and shovel." Lord, this woman was good. Damn good at twisting a story to fit her needs. He'd have to remember how well she could spin a yarn.

"What's your pa's name, Annabelle?"

"John McKenzie," she said innocently.

William frowned. "I once had a bounty hunter named James McKenzie chasing my ass. Any relation?"

She smiled and nodded. "That's the crazy branch of the family—my father's brother. Those people are as loony as sheepherders, and since there have been times we've had to straddle both sides of the law, we avoid them like an outbreak of the plague. We don't need that kind of trouble."

Beau held his breath as he watched William thinking about what Annabelle had just told him. If the man didn't believe her, they were as good as dead. And he didn't know if he could outdraw William. The man was fast as lightening with a gun.

William smiled at Annabelle. "Nice to meet you, Annabelle. As long as Beau can find the money, we're good."

A quiet sigh of relief whooshed from Beau's lungs. It appeared the outlaw was buying her story. Once Beau made it to Fort Worth, he was going to check out the McKenzies and see what he could learn about Annabelle's family.

"Oh, he'll find that money. Our share is going to set up our home. And then he'll have to earn more."

The men all laughed. "Welcome to married life."

Beau nodded and took the good-natured ribbing. Annabelle had done well. For a moment there, he'd been afraid they would recognize her family, but she'd turned that to their advantage. He was pleased with how well she'd done. Even he was beginning to believe her sisters were bounty hunters.

"I guess I'm hogtied with matrimonial ropes," Beau said, giving Annabelle a teasing smile.

"Oh, honey," she said. "You'll be doing good if those ropes aren't real."

The woman could play the game. Now, if he could just get the two of them out of here safely.

*

Darkness had fallen, and Annabelle hated the fact she didn't move more than five feet away from Beau. The men gazed at her like they could see right through her clothes and knew the size and shape of her pantaloons. The situation was making her nervous, and she knew Beau was watching them, so she'd stayed close to her make-believe husband.

She'd added some canned peaches to the outlaw's meal, and they'd looked at her like she was a goddess for about five minutes, and then the mood had returned to them watching her and Beau. A chill had spread itself into her bones, leaving her jumpy and as nervous as a dog dreaming of catching a rabbit.

She feared that once they located the money, they'd both be dead.

"Annabelle, do you have any sisters?" Tom asked.

She licked her lips, fear for them chugging through

her veins like whiskey. "Nope, I'm an only child."

Beau frowned and she smiled. "My maw she died when I was real young, and my pa, he never remarried. So I'm alone."

Her sisters couldn't be far behind, but she wasn't about to endanger her family. She'd lie to protect them and hope they rode in and saved her from the Harris gang, but most of all Beau. He was tempting as sin on a Sunday morning. And she was doing her best not to let her heart think about the contours of his muscles and the way he smiled when he was pleased or his large emerald eyes. He was heartache with a side dish of misery.

"Darn shame. We'd go back to Zenith and find your sisters if they're as pretty as you are."

She smiled. "Sorry to disappoint you, gentlemen. Tell me about your wives. What can I expect when we get to Crockett?"

Anything to keep them from talking about her or noticing her. Maybe by thinking of home, they would remember their own wives and girlfriends.

William shrugged, his eyes lingering on Annabelle. "Only two of us are married. Now three," he said, glancing over at Beau. "You've never lived in Crockett with the rest of us, have you?"

"No, the time we've been together has always been on the trail."

The discussion swung away from wives and girlfriends. Still, Annabelle didn't feel any better about the conversation. Why did it seem to revolve around her and Beau just like the outlaws' gazes seemed to focus on the two of them? A tingly sensation of danger was never far from her.

William laughed, but his smile didn't reach his cold

dark eyes. "Tell me again, what banks you robbed. I've forgotten."

"I told you when I first joined the gang," Beau said, his voice tough.

"So remind me," William said. "I want to hear it again."

"Dublin, Wichita, Fort Griffin, and Tyler. That last one about got me killed. It was either join up with a group of men or die trying to make a living," Beau said, staring at the fire.

His jaw twitched, and for a moment, she wasn't certain he was telling the truth. There was something about his story that didn't seem right. Or was that just wishful thinking on her part? Did she want him so badly she hoped this was all just some big misunderstanding?

God, she was a hopeless romantic, and it would serve her well to remember Beau Samuel was a man wanted for robbery. A man she intended to turn in and collect the ransom for, if they made it out of here alive.

"That's quite a record. How come I'd never heard of you before?"

"I don't know. A wanted poster is hanging in almost every town I go in, offering a five hundred dollar reward."

Yet, the Beau she'd come to know was different from the rough and rugged men who sat around the campfire. These men's eyes were cold. Their dark expressions never changed, and if any man had a sweetheart waiting for him, she'd be surprised. What had made them the cruel, ruthless killers they obviously were?

Maybe she didn't want to know. Sometimes there were things that were better left alone, and these were the type of men she avoided. Their souls were so damaged only God could salvage them. She prayed Beau could get them out of here before these callous men decided they no longer needed them.

"The wanted poster is in my saddlebags," Annabelle volunteered and then quickly realized there were other posters besides Beau's in there. She didn't need them finding those.

"No, sugar, I used it to start last night's fire," Beau said, with a smile that told her he had read her mind.

"That's right. After that downpour, we couldn't find any dry kindling."

"Five hundred. That's impressive," William said, an evil grin spread across his face and Annabelle felt a shiver go through her. "That would make a nice haul along with the bank money if we were to turn you in."

Beau shrugged like it meant nothing, but Annabelle could see the way his body tensed. He was trying to keep calm. It was all she could do to keep from running, jumping on her horse, and riding away. She didn't like these men. She didn't want to stay here a moment longer.

"It would. But I figure it's best we all stay out of jail. That way, no one is spilling the beans about locations and who all is involved in the hold-ups," he warned.

William picked up a stick and pulled out his knife. In less than a minute, he'd fashioned himself a toothpick. "Keeping information to yourself is always good if you want to live."

Silence hung dark and heavy around the campfire. Annabelle noticed that one of the men was staring at her more than the others, his dark eyes piercing her as if he'd like nothing better than to knife her. It was almost as if his gaze was stabbing her with his hatred and suspicion.

"Where did you get those peaches?" he finally asked,

the frown on his face filled with loathing.

"My pa has peach trees on his farm. He sent them with me for our new home," she said, trying to keep the nervous tremor out of her voice. Why would he be angry about peaches?

"That farmer we killed last night, he served us canned peaches with our dinner. Those peaches tasted exactly like these." He spit on the ground at her feet.

Annabelle's heart skipped a beat, and then she smiled at the man. "Really? I couldn't tell you the first thing about canning peaches. My pa refused to let me in the kitchen after I burned it down. He did all the cooking, and he loved canning peaches."

The men around the campfire chuckled.

"You see what you're getting yourself shackled with, Beau. The woman can't even cook," William said, as he pulled out his gun, pointed it at Annabelle, and pulled back the trigger. "Where did you get those peaches, girl?"

Her heart slammed into her chest, and she gasped. Within thirty seconds, anger flooded her. She put her hands on her hips and stared at William's gun. Her heart was galloping as fast as a racehorse. Her hands were shaking, but she'd hidden them by putting them on her waist.

"Good grief," she said. "If this is the kind of thanks I get for sharing my pa's peaches, then I'll just keep the next jar to myself. What farmer are you talking about?"

Though she'd seen Beau move his hand to his gun, he hadn't said a word. She glanced at him. His eyes had darkened, and she knew he was angry. If he lost his temper, then they were just as good as dead. Oh, they'd keep him alive until they found the money, but they'd kill her in a second, and he wouldn't be long afterwards.

William slowly put his gun back in his holster, shook his head, and sighed. "Don't worry about it. He was a jackass who didn't want to share his horses. So we took them."

Annabelle smiled and took a deep breath. "I just hate jackasses. They're so dumb."

They'd shot that poor farmer over his horses and then burned his home to the ground. These sadistic savages would just as soon shoot a man if they thought he would betray them. She swallowed, her stomach tight with fear and nausea. Her and Beau were in so much danger.

"Beau, honey, don't you think it's time we called it a night? I'm kind of missing the feel of your sweet arms around me," she said, as she stared at him with a smile. She had to get him to smile or act like nothing was wrong. If he stayed angry, they were going to die.

The men snickered.

"You better take advantage of her wanting to spend the night with you. As soon as the honeymoon is over, she'll be complaining and pushing you out of bed. Enjoy it while you can," William said, watching the interaction between the two of them.

Annabelle's knees were knocking beneath her skirt. She knew she had to appear like she was unafraid, but she didn't know how much longer she could continue this charade.

Beau stood and walked to Annabelle's side. "Night, gentleman." His voice was curt, and he didn't respond to William.

They walked a short distance from the fire.

"You newlyweds don't go too far," William said. "I'm setting up a sentry to keep guard. We don't need any surprises during the night."

Annabelle knew the sentry was protecting all of them, but mainly making certain her and Beau didn't slink off in the night. William may not seem too bright, but he was a cautious man—a man who didn't leave anything to chance. And he wasn't about to let her and Beau slip off in the middle of the night. It was a subtle warning, but a warning just the same.

"You can't get angry," Annabelle whispered, slipping her arm around his waist as they walked away from the circle of men. He put his arm around her shoulders and pulled her in close.

Beau's mouth had a hard edge around it, like he was gritting his teeth. "The man pulled a gun on my wife. What am I suppose to do? Sing and dance?"

"Your make-believe wife." She watched as a muscle twitched in his jaw. "You pretend nothing is wrong, or we both die. Your choice."

He made a snarling face at her. "I don't like anyone threatening what's mine."

She laid her hand on his arm and gazed up into his green eyes like he was the man who had stolen her heart. She could be a consummate actress when their lives were on the line. And right now, she knew one wrong move and they'd both be dead.

"Honey," she said and ran her hand over Beau's chest, leaning in close. "They're watching us. They're making sure we're a happily married couple who are going to sleep in each other's arms tonight."

Together, they made a spectacle of spreading out their one-and-only bedroll.

"That being said, I want you to put a blanket between us tonight. Don't even think about cuddling up next to me," she whispered.

"The hell I'm not," he said, standing close to her ear. "We're newlyweds. We'd be all over each other like a bear to a honey tree. And there are no extra blankets."

"But we're not really married."

"You have to pretend," he said, and his lips turned up in a smile.

For a moment, she wanted to double up her fists and hit him, but she knew it wouldn't look good for a couple of newlyweds to already be fighting.

"Damn you, Beau," she said real sweetly with a smile on her face. "It's not nice to throw a woman's words back at her."

He laughed softly in her ear. "Do you want to live?"

She nodded, knowing it was true. Her life was ahead of her. She wanted to have a good man's arms around her, get married, and have a family. Hell, she even wanted to return to the farm and raise her children there and talk to the chickens again. They'd probably stopped laying eggs because she wasn't there urging them to get their business done.

"Then keep playing the game. We've got to convince them we're a happy married couple."

"When this is over, I'm going to insist my sisters have my brain examined for being crazy."

Annabelle was never one for rash decisions, and this was the reason why. She'd jeopardized so much when she'd followed Beau, trying to prove to her sisters she was just as capable as they were. That she could bring in a bounty on her own.

"If we're still alive, you won't need a doctor to tell your sisters you're loony. I'll do it in person," he said. "I'll tell them how you followed me like a bitch in heat."

"Hrmph," she said. "You can tell them from your jail cell, but they'll never believe you."

Chapter Six

Beau lay in his bedroll, grateful to once again be sleeping on something other than the hard ground. But he feared he'd get very little, if any, rest tonight. Annabelle stood over him, frowning down at the blankets. He motioned for her to join him and she scowled. Good Lord, the woman was the one who'd mentioned them sleeping together, and now she was having second thoughts. Reservations that could get them killed. And while she was ornery enough to drive a sane man to drink, he wasn't ready to meet his maker just yet. There were things he'd yet to accomplish.

If his mother were to find out there was a wanted poster with his picture on it, she'd be happy to see he was following in his brothers' footsteps, but angry he wasn't going after northern banks. His brothers had names known well enough to scare men away. So he didn't utter Jesse's or Frank's name to anyone.

"Would you get your pretty little self down here," he said, looking up at her. "Or am I going to have to toss you onto these blankets?"

That was an image he didn't need in his head right now. Tossing Annabelle onto the blankets and covering her body with his. Just the idea of the feel of her womanly curves against him was enough to have his blood pumping like a stampede of cattle.

She shook her head, sunk to her knees, and then lay beside him, pushing her skirts down. "You've obviously never worn a skirt with petticoats beneath it, or you'd know that if you're not careful, they can balloon out around you."

"Nope, I've never worn petticoats. Can't get a seamstress to make them in my size," he said, laughing into her ear, trying to get his raging hard-on under control. "But I don't think that was the problem."

Now that he had her on the ground, he was sorry there were so many men around. He'd love to spend the night nuzzling on her earlobe, putting his nose against her sweet neck, and breathing in her essence. Already his dick was harder than stone, and this was certainly not the time or the place for his shaft to wake up to the soft, engaging smell of the woman next to him.

He pulled the blanket up over them and snuggled in next to her. It was then he felt the outline of a gun hidden in her petticoats. A sense of danger prickled the back of his neck. "When were you planning on using that gun on me? Were you going to shoot me in the back?"

"My pa taught me to always be prepared to defend my honor." She shrugged. "I've been just waiting for my sisters to catch up to us, and then you would have seen my petticoat pistol."

The idea of her sisters threatening him and her pulling her pistol on him was daunting, but he'd never let her know. Laughing, he shook his head. "And here I thought you were a prim and proper young miss."

"Ha! If I were a prim and proper young woman, I

never would have had to take a job as a waitress who had to dump food on men to get them to behave. I'd be married and have a whole passel of kids by now. Besides, high-falutin women are boring. One thing I'm not is dull."

"No, you're definitely not boring or dull." Beau pulled her up against his chest and wrapped his arm around her. "Sometimes what makes us stronger prepares us for what life throws at us."

He thought about his own past and how dealing with his outlaw brothers was what made him into the man he was today.

"What would you know about being a woman forced to find a job to survive?"

"I don't, but I do know about people thinking you're something you're not."

For a moment, Beau was afraid he'd revealed too much. But since he was a young boy and his two brothers made a name for themselves as America's most wanted outlaws, people had expected him to be cut of the same cloth. And while they had the same blood, that didn't mean he was the meanest hombre south of the border. Jesse and Frank held that title.

Her breathing slowed, and he could tell she was thinking about what he'd just said. "Besides, being a waitress taught you how to deal with men."

"Being a waitress improved my sharp-shooter skills. I can nail a can or a man from fifty yards."

While he thought the idea of her nailing a can funny, he didn't want to be the one she was aiming for. He laughed, reached down, and pulled up her petticoats.

"What are you doing?"

"I'm removing your gun," he said.

"Don't even think about it or these outlaws are going to witness our first marital fight," she warned him.

His hand hovered about her holster. He wanted to take that gun away, but knew there would be a fight. Okay, maybe now was not the time to divest her of that sweet little pistol. But the opportunity would come sooner or later, and she'd find herself with an empty holster.

"But, honey, thanks to you they think we're ten yards away from them making love," he said nuzzling her neck, breathing in her sweet scent, and feeling himself growing harder by the second.

"Don't think about that either," she cautioned.

"You brought it up," he said, teasing. Maybe right now they needed to keep things light, so the men around them would think they were adorable newlyweds.

"And I can feel just how excited you got at the idea. Pretend you're asleep."

"That's going to be difficult." He let out a pent-up frustrated sigh.

She laughed and fell silent. Yet, he could feel her heart pounding in her chest and her soft breathing. Finally, she asked, "Do you think we're going to get out of this alive?"

"All we can do is try," he told her, not really certain himself. "But you did real good today. Even when that outrider asked you about the peaches."

"That was too close," she said.

"You handled it well."

"Why, thank you, Mr. Samuel. Coming from an experienced outlaw like yourself, that's a real compliment, I think."

He frowned. There was no reason for her words to

irritate him, but they did. He didn't like it when she called him an outlaw. He didn't like it when she compared him to the men of the gang, yet that's what he was. An outlaw on the run, with no need for a woman by his side, even a beautiful, soft, willing woman. "You better get some sleep."

"That's going to be difficult. I'm in a real precarious position here. I have a man behind me with a loaded weapon in his pants and a band of outlaws surrounding me. Could you sleep?" she asked, her voice taut with nerves.

A chuckle rumbled from his chest. *His weapon* was loaded and just needing a signal from her to unload into her sweet, womanly body. He kissed the back of her neck. "If those outlaws weren't surrounding us, no, we wouldn't be sleeping. We'd be doing what all married couples do."

"But we aren't married," she said quietly.

"No, but you said we could pretend."

And Good Lord, he wanted to feign they were man and wife and celebrating their wedding night. He wanted to bury himself so deep in her she'd be begging him. Yet, it was all a sweet lie that was just a temptation that interfered with his focus and kept him off kilter.

"And then you'd leave me, possibly with a bun in the oven. Just what a woman needs. More heartache and a baby to raise with an absent father, a man wanted by the law. No, thank you."

No, he didn't want a child brought into this world without him being with the mother and child. A father was important to a boy or girl. There would be no children raised without him.

"You really do like to put a damper on things, don't

you?"

"That's my job. I'm always the reliable, sensible sister. Always looking out for my sisters, never thinking of myself. Never the one who takes risks or does things that put me in jeopardy," she said with a sigh. "Until now."

In the darkness, his brows drew together in a frown. An uneasy sense of fate overcame him.

"So what happened to bring you out of your shell? Your boyfriend break your heart and you decided to get even?" he asked, wondering what had caused Annabelle to choose to follow him out of town. She didn't sound like a woman who risked everything on a whim.

"Nope, nothing so romantic. Just the need to catch one last bounty to end my sisters traveling days. Only it didn't work out like I thought it would."

A snicker escaped his lips. "No, it didn't." He paused, the idea of two more women who looked like Annabelle searching for her disheartening. "How far behind do you think your sisters are?"

He didn't want two more women to protect from the Harris gang. Two more women they would think were a gift to satisfy their lust.

"I don't know. I would have thought they would have caught us by now. But maybe they've taken a wrong turn or something. I'm worried about them. I don't want to be riding with the Harris gang when they locate me. It could get ugly."

"Yeah, that wouldn't be good. Go to sleep, Annabelle. Shut your eyes and try to get some sleep. Tomorrow could be a long day," he said, worried about what the morrow would bring.

"What are you going to do?" she asked.

"I'll be awake, listening and watching."

"Good night, Beau."

Why did her words, the sound of her voice, send warm ripples through him? Why was he even more worried now than ever before? How could he secure the money, protect Annabelle, and get them both out of here alive?

For the first time ever, he regretted the decisions he'd made with regards to his own life. There were times he wished he could be the kind of man who settled down with a woman and a family. Being with Annabelle made him regret the choices he'd made.

*

Later that night, Annabelle awoke with an insistent need to find a bush and relieve her long, denied bladder. She'd not gone to the bushes since they'd joined the Harris gang for fear of some outlaw walking up on her with her bloomers down.

Slowly, she tried to rise without waking Beau, who breathed deeply and evenly. The arm that had been wrapped around her, like he was shielding her, dropped to the ground. She stood and walked away from the dying campfire and the sacked out outlaws into the dark. Quiet as possible, she stepped into the shadows away from the men.

Hurriedly, she did her business. Once she was finished, she started to walk back into the camp when she heard the voices. Slinking down behind the bushes, she watched in the glow of the dying campfire as William and Tom stood talking quietly. They had not been there when she'd left the camp area.

William was giving Tom direction. "At first light, we'll leave. Let's plan on reaching the Red River tomorrow, instead of the day after like Beau thinks. Then we can have him locate the money the day after tomorrow, and by sundown, he'll be staring at the sky seeing nothing."

"Do you think it's necessary to kill him?" the night sentry asked.

"He says he's robbed all those banks, but I got that tingling in my gut that's warning me he's dangerous. Besides, it'll mean more of the share for each of us." William lit a rolled cigarette and took a deep puff.

The sentry nodded. "Yeah, I'd like to have his part of the robbery money. What about his wife?"

Annabelle held her breath, fear filling her as her imagination ran wild with what they would do to her once Beau was dead. God, she would never ever stray from home again, if only she could find her way back.

"I'm sure you boys will enjoy her, and then we can send her off to purgatory to meet up with her husband."

"Yeah, I'd like to get a piece of that fluff. I still think they found that farmer. Those were the same peaches," he said, his voice rising. "She lied."

Annabelle cursed the peaches she'd taken from the root cellar. How could a jar of fruit cause so much trouble? A shiver traveled down her spine at the realization they were going to kill them both.

"I didn't notice until you mentioned it. But I think you're right."

"The spices were the same. Not everyone puts cloves in their peaches, and those had the same spice as the ones that farmer fed us the night before."

William took another drag on his cigarette and blew the smoke out slowly. "She can certainly talk her way out of a situation. Now, I'm questioning whether or not they're really married. Has he ever mentioned a woman before?"

"Never."

Silence filled the night for several moments, and Annabelle stood in one spot, not moving, hoping they wouldn't discover her hiding behind the bushes. An owl hooted nearby, and the cold night air had her shivering. She had to make it back to Beau.

"Is she wearing a wedding ring?" the sentry asked William.

"I don't remember seeing one," William said, squatting down on his haunches and stirring the fire. "I'll look first thing in the morning. If I discover they're not married, I'll torture the location from him, and then we'll dump the bodies and move on. In the meantime, keep a watch out so they don't get away." He rose from the fire.

"Will do."

The two men strolled off into the darkness, and Annabelle breathed a sigh of relief. She stayed where she was for a long time, waiting, her knees knocking, longing for her bed at home. An ache filled her chest, and a yearning for her sisters brought tears to her eyes. She wanted to go home to the donkeys braying and those damn chickens scratching in the dirt and clucking when they saw her coming. She'd never curse their existence again.

In the dark, she sat there waiting, willing her sisters to find her, rescue her and take her home. A half hour later, she crept from her hiding place and slipped back into their bedroll.

"Where in the hell have you been?" Beau whispered, his voice harsh. "I was about to go searching for you."

She curled toward him, their faces inches away from

each other. "We've got to get out of here, tonight."

"Why? What happened?"

"I went to the bushes and overheard them talking. Those damn peaches made them suspicious. Now, they're talking of killing us and questioning whether or not we're married. They're going to look for a ring on my hand in the morning," she murmured, trying to keep the panic out of her voice as it pulsed through her veins.

"Lots of women don't wear rings. That's hardly a reason for them to be suspicious."

"You can stay if you want to, but I'm out of here before dawn. I'm not sticking around to watch them torture the truth out of you. Your life ain't worth penny candy right now. You're a dead man and don't even know it," she said, trying to conceal her frustration with Beau, wanting to scream this knowledge at him, knowing they had to leave tonight.

"Slow down and tell me exactly what they said."

God, he was so patient. So damn exacting, when all she wanted to do was for the two of them to ride until there was a safe distance between them and this gang of ruthless outlaws.

Annabelle whispered everything she'd heard to Beau. He listened carefully, and when she was finished, he was silent.

"I'm leaving," she said quietly, pulling up the covers and settling in.

"And just how do you plan on sneaking out of here?"

"Men are stupid. While you saddle the horses, I'll take care of the watchman."

Beau could do what he wanted, but she was riding out of here in an hour, two at the most, and leaving this gang of cutthroats behind. She wasn't ready to die. No amount of bounty money was worth her life.

"Now is not the time for us to discuss your falsehoods about men. Still, I don't like this plan."

"Do you have a better one?" she asked.

He was silent and then she heard him sigh. "No."

"Okay, then. I'll lure the watchman into the bushes, while you saddle the horses," she said, knowing she could entice the watchman into his downfall. He'd follow her if he saw her going into the bushes, and she'd be waiting with her pistol in hand.

"Are you sure about this?" Beau asked.

"Honey, a man like him thinks with only one part of his anatomy, and when I was a waitress, I learned years ago how to cool men off. Let's just say he'll have one hell of a headache in the morning."

"If you don't show up in five minutes, I'm coming for you."

"Just have the horses saddled and ready to go."

"Try to get some rest. We need these guys to sleep while we're slipping away. They'll come after us," he warned.

Oh yeah, they'd come after them. The chase would be on, and they'd be searching for her and Beau. If they were caught, they were dead.

"I'd rather die trying to escape them than watch while they inflict pain on you. You may be a ruthless outlaw, but you're still a man who doesn't deserve to be tortured," she said, knowing she would capitulate before she'd let him suffer.

"You'd rather see me hang?"

No, she didn't want to watch him hang. She couldn't bear the thought of a rope around his neck and him swinging from a tree, but what was she supposed to do?

Choose him over her sisters' well-being?

"You're a lot of trouble, but you're my bounty. I'm looking to collect that five hundred dollars, not watch them torture you to death."

She wasn't brave. She was as weak as they came, and the idea of anyone being deliberately hurt or injured would have her screaming out whatever it was they wanted to know. She'd last about two seconds, and then they'd kill her, just to shut her up.

He rolled to his back. "I'm not liking this one bit."

"Do you like pain?"

"No."

"Then we're leaving."

*

An hour later, Annabelle rolled up their bedroll and handed it to Beau.

"I still don't like this," he whispered.

"Then stay, I'm leaving," she said, knowing they had to get away. Fear pulsed through her veins like the scotch whiskey she occasionally sipped with her sisters.

She'd bluffed her way out of the gang's questions yesterday, but if they were to hurt Beau, she'd confess. She'd confess everything and probably some things she'd never done, just to save him from being hurt.

"You've got five minutes," Beau said. "Then I'm coming in after you."

"Fine, but wait until I lure him in, before you start counting," she said. Good grief, the man didn't have any faith in her abilities to ensnare stupid men. This, she could do.

She pulled out the little pot of lipstick she carried with her. Just a dash of the color would make her feel more enticing.

"What the hell is that?" Beau said in a loud whisper.

"Lipstick."

He shook his head, a frown on his face. "Is that necessary?"

"You bet it is," she said, feeling closer to her sisters. "It's my calling card."

"Just get this over with and let's get out of here."

She smiled at him, turned, and walked away, swaying her hips as she went, letting him get some idea of her trap. She strolled to the edge of the camp, turned her head, and glanced back over her shoulder at the sentry who was watching her. His brows drew together in a frown.

Annabelle smiled at him and winked. She didn't know if he'd see her eye twitch in the dark, but she hoped it was enough to get him to follow her. If not, she'd come back and motion him into the darkness.

Hurrying through the bushes, she found a tree to hide behind, pulled out her gun and waited. In less than a minute, the sound of a snapping twig alerted her someone approached. And she'd bet her next meal the sentry was near.

God, men were so predictable. But then women, other than her sisters, you could foretell when they'd take their next breath. They were boring and silly and difficult to be around. When Ruby was expelled from school, Annabelle had secretly rejoiced that her sister wasn't an ordinary woman. She liked that she was different. Unusual. Not conventional.

But then, all three of the McKenzie sisters had been called unusual on many occasions.

Through the bushes, she watched the man as he walked toward her and she held her breath. She had a surprise waiting for him. And not what he was hoping he'd find in the bushes with her.

He made her job so easy. He stopped with his back to her, and she took the butt of her gun and whacked him hard on the head.

"Damn," he said, wheeling around to face her. Holding his head, he weaved and fell to the ground with a loud thump. She breathed a sigh of relief. There for a moment she'd feared he was not going to pass out, and she would have to fight him. Her whack on the head had taken a moment longer than she'd liked to take effect.

She grabbed his arm and dragged him out of the path. Pulling out a piece of rope she'd stashed earlier in her pocket, she quickly tied him to the tree. Forcing his jaws open, she stuffed a rag in his mouth and then stood back and admired her handiwork.

Not bad for a chicken wrangler who took care of the farm. Not bad for a newbie bounty hunter without experience. Not bad for a girl scared out of her wits and just wanting to get away.

She sighed, releasing the fear that had gripped her insides like a case of food poisoning. Sure, she'd been confident with Beau, but that didn't mean she wasn't afraid. She'd been scared enough she'd worried he would hear the pounding of her heart.

But she was done and it was time to rejoin Beau.

Lifting her skirts, she ran back down the path to where the horses were tied. Hopefully, he'd have them ready to ride. When she came around the corner, he was standing there frowning, waiting on her.

"About time you got here," he whispered.

"Oh, shut up and let's go."

"Is it done?"

101

She wanted to reply something sarcastic and witty, but didn't have time to think. They needed to ride and quick. "He won't be bothering us for a while. He's got a goose egg on his head, and he's all tied up, taking a little forced nap."

Beau smiled at her and shook his head. "God, you scare me, woman."

"I should," she said with bravo, knowing that really she was just a big pussy cat who when petted would purr happily. But mess with her or her sisters and she could turn into a tiger.

"Let's go," he said and handed her the reins to her horse.

She glanced around, frowning, knowing once they rode off, the gang would be right behind them. They'd be riding hell bent in the dark. Not exactly the safest ride. "Wait."

"What?" he said, his voice rising above a whisper.

"We're making it too easy for them to follow us."

Walking to the other horses, she untied each one. When Beau realized what she was doing, he joined her. He slapped the horse on the buttocks and the animal took off running. By the time all the horses were racing away, the camp was beginning to stir.

"Hey, what are you doing?" a deep, sleepy voice yelled.

"Come on," Beau whispered.

Annabelle slapped the last horse on the butt and then climbed on her own animal. Men were calling out, asking what was going on.

Together, they took off at a run, and the other horses followed them. She smiled. Now the Harris gang had no way of following them.

A gunshot blasted the night air. She felt a bullet whirr by her head. Leaning over her horse, she spurred him on into the night. Into the darkness.

Excitement of getting away spiraled through her. Maybe being a bounty hunter wasn't so bad after all. Then the rational part of her laughed. No, she couldn't wait to get home to her boring life. It was safer.

Chapter Seven

Meg glanced over at her husband and frowned. So far, the honeymoon was dreadful. She was worried sick about Annabelle. They'd spent the last three days searching for her sister with Ruby's help. And while she loved both her sisters, being alone with her new husband would have been great. It was kind of hard to experience the loving touch of his arms when Ruby slept less than five yards away. *And with Annabelle still missing.*

In fact, it was impossible. Meg was worried sick about Annabelle, and Ruby insisted on going with them to locate their missing sibling. Meg couldn't blame her. She would have laughed if Ruby suggested Meg sit at home, while Ruby searched for their wayward sister.

They were family. She'd do whatever was necessary to save Annabelle because she couldn't for a moment think she might be dead. Meg believed Annabelle was still alive. She had to be. And they had to locate her.

They traveled slowly, stopping at every small farm to ask if Annabelle had been seen. Until late yesterday afternoon, they'd had no luck, but then they'd come across a muddied A in the dirt with an arrow. Meg could only hope Annabelle was leaving them a message, and that gave her hope.

This morning they rode down the lane of a farmhouse. There were no barking dogs, no sounds greeted them, even the birds seemed to have deserted the property. When they rounded a curve in the lane, she saw the burned out farmhouse.

"That's not good," Zach said, gazing worriedly at the property. "You girls wait here."

"No," Ruby said. "We're going with you."

"Why do I even try to protect you two?" Zach asked, shaking his head.

Meg smiled. "Someday you'll learn we're not your usual helpless women."

They halted their horses in the yard. Meg knew Zach wanted only to protect her and Ruby, but giving total control over to a man, even the man she loved with every fiber of her being, was tough. It was something the newlyweds were grappling with.

"How's your ankle holding up?" Meg asked Ruby, not wanting her running around on the sprain.

"It's sore, but I'll make it. Don't worry about me."

"Ha, I always worry about you."

Ruby raised her brows at her older sister. "That's your problem, not mine."

She was still angry that Meg was getting out of the bounty hunting business. But she'd get over it and soon learn to settle down, once they found Annabelle. Meg was giving up chasing bad men to settle down and enjoy her husband and live her dream of owning a dress shop.

Zach dropped to the ground and turned to help his wife, who had already alighted from her horse.

He shook his head at her. "Stay close."

"Sure," Meg said and then walked in the direction of

the back of the house.

"I'm sure glad I'm the man of the house," Zach said beneath his breath.

Meg turned and smiled at him. "Cowboy, in the bedroom you are the man, but out on the trail, we're equal."

He shook his head at her. "It wouldn't do me any good to argue with you, would it?"

"Nope," she said with a laugh and winked at him before she focused on locating clues that her sister had been here. It was difficult to hold back not being excited to be near her husband, yet so frightened for Annabelle. Once they located her missing sister, they could focus on their new life together. Then she could enjoy her husband.

Zach walked around the burned out structure, while Meg wandered in the opposite direction. She found the door to the root cellar and opened it. Peering down inside, she could see where canned goods had been removed from the dusty shelves, leaving rings showing jars were missing.

Climbing down inside the cellar, she walked around the small area. On a shelf hidden from view, an A appeared in the dust. Her sister had been here. Knowing Annabelle, she'd taken the canned goods because she'd left without any supplies. Now, at least she had food.

Ruby yelled. "Hey, I found it."

Meg hurriedly climbed out of the root cellar and raced toward Ruby's voice. Zach and Meg arrived at the same time at Ruby's side. There in the dirt was the letter A and an arrow pointing back down the lane. Annabelle had been here, but she was gone. But what had happened and why was the farmhouse still smoldering?

"There's a fresh grave back behind the house," Zach said. "And the fire didn't happen that long ago."

What if that grave was Annabelle's?

Meg reached out and touched her husband's arm for strength. Their eyes met and held for a moment.

"No," he said. "She couldn't have left us this message if she was dead."

She sighed with relief. He was right. She had to be alive. She just had to be.

"The root cellar has been gone through," Meg said. "There was an A scratched in the dust on the shelf."

"See, she's alive," Zach assured her.

"There's no livestock?" Ruby said. "No animals. I don't know a farmer who doesn't at least have chickens."

"Yeah," Zach replied. "Something happened and whatever it was, the place has been cleaned out."

"Let's get going," Meg said. "I feel like we're close."

"At least we know we're on her trail."

They crawled up on their horses and rode down the lane on the prowl once again for Annabelle.

*

Beau kept them off the main path. Sure, they had escaped from the ruthless gang of outlaws, but he wasn't taking any chances they would be located. If the gang found them again, William wouldn't hesitate to shoot. Oh, he'd wait until he learned the location of the money, but once he gained that knowledge, they would be breathing their last breaths.

Beau had to locate the money and then get them to Fort Worth, where hopefully they would be given protection.

Slowing their horses to let them rest, they watched the sky turn purple with the rays of the rising sun.

Nothing was more beautiful than witnessing the dawn of a new day. It never failed to fill him with awe, and he always thought of his family, especially his mother telling him God was blessing him with a new day.

"How long have you been a member of the Harris gang?" Annabelle asked.

"Long enough," he said, not wanting to reveal too much. He sighed. Annabelle was not stupid by any means, and she certainly realized there were some incongruences in his relationship with the Harris gang.

"That wasn't an answer. That was you telling me you don't want me to know."

He chuckled. The less she knew the better.

"Only a month or so. We've robbed a couple of banks together is all," he responded.

Her forehead drew together in a frown like she was thinking hard. "They certainly don't seem to trust you. Has it always been this way or did you do something to make them angry?"

Oh, he'd done more than they knew, but still, he didn't want Annabelle to know. He'd tell her what she already knew and hope it was enough to satisfy her curiosity.

He shook his head. "A posse was on our tail. We scattered, and I rode off with the bank money, saving it. I guess the gang would have been happier if I'd stuck around, and we could have all gotten arrested."

"No, it's more than that. You don't seem to fit in with them. You're not as cold-blooded or maybe you hide it better than they do. Or something. "

He laughed. He had to scare her, make her think he was a monster because if they were caught again, the gang would hurt her. The less she knew about Beau the better off she'd be. While he was trying very hard not to like Annabelle, she was a woman who reminded him of his sisters and his family. He could tumble into forever with her if he wasn't careful.

"Sugar, don't be making me out to be a nice guy who's going to whisk you off to the preacher man and promise you a house and kids. Nope, the law is looking for me, and they have a rope with my name on it."

Maybe that would keep her off the trail he didn't want her pursuing, though he doubted it. She was a stubborn woman who saw way more than he wanted to reveal.

"Yeah, I know. But I don't know of a single outlaw who would have buried a man and his son. Or said a prayer over their dead bodies. Or not taken advantage of me last night. You're acting like a nice guy," she said, staring at him, her sapphire eyes questioning.

Those blue eyes were way too knowing and curious. How could he throw her off the trail? How could he convince her he was one mean ass hombre?

"So do you want me to kill someone and prove to you that I'm an outlaw? Even an outlaw says prayers because we have a tendency to die younger than most men," he said in such a flippant way that even he cringed.

"No, I don't believe you. Most don't say prayers because they know their soul is going straight to hell."

"Well, I'm certainly glad Saint Peter put you here on earth to decide our fates." His stomach burned like he'd eaten a bushel of jalapenos. Memories rushed at him. "You don't know the reason why most men become outlaws. In my case, my family was forced off our farm. I followed my older brother's footsteps."

What he'd told her was the truth, and yet, there was

so much more hidden in his words. How a family member could rip out your soul and leave you to die.

She frowned at him. "Where's your brother now?"

He shrugged. "We parted ways years ago."

Somehow he'd managed to stay alive after Jesse had all but vanquished him from the family. In the last few days, being with Annabelle had brought up so much of his anger at his past. Why did this fluff of a woman have him thinking of what he'd walked away from?

"When you parted ways, why didn't you give up being an outlaw?"

Though his mother had wanted him to, he'd never actually ridden with Frank and Jesse. He'd wandered the plains, until he'd found a chance to get even with his brothers. "And do what?"

"Get another farm," she said.

With surprise, he realized he missed the farm. He'd been fifteen when they'd been forced to leave. At first, he'd been happy he no longer had the chores to do. But then he'd missed his animals. His mother had been devastated, and his sisters got married and moved away. At first, Jesse had been a hero of the war, but slowly, his reputation as a ruthless killer had turned public sentiment against him. And with that rising tide of hate, the town had come to despise the family, even though his mother had remarried years before.

Eventually, Beau had left town filled with anger at his brothers and left feeling rejected by the family. Until he found his current profession.

"Farming is a lot of hard work. Robbing a bank is easier."

"Hrmph. Except that you're stealing from someone and it's against the law."

He shrugged. "Not unless you get caught. I don't plan on getting caught."

She laughed. "Sugar," she said, mocking him. "You're caught. You just won't accept it yet."

"You and what posse?" he asked, staring at her and wishing he could kiss that sweet, luscious mouth of hers and knowing that wouldn't be a good idea. This woman fired his blood like no one else. Touching her mouth could send him over the edge. They'd soon come to with little or no clothes between them and his seed planted in her belly. No, she may not be an innocent, but he didn't want any children without him there to help in their raising.

She opened her mouth to respond when he heard the sound of hooves behind them.

"Shh," he said, cutting her off. Terror ran up his spine at the sound of pounding hoofs on the hard ground.

"Don't tell me to *shh*," she replied, and then she apparently heard the noise, for her eyes widened with fear.

"Come on, let's hide in the trees," he told her, directing his horse off the path and into the bushes.

Quickly, he pulled them into a grove that had enough brush to hide them and the horses. He jumped off his mount, pulling out his gun. Annabelle slid off her mustang. Her saddle twisted, and she stopped to tighten the cinch with her back to the approaching riders.

A flash of red hair beneath a black hat caught his attention and then a blonde wearing a calico dress. A lawman rode with them.

Oh no, it was her bounty hunter sisters and a sheriff. If she spotted them, he wouldn't be able to keep her quiet. He had to distract her.

He would be as good as dead if her sisters caught him.

Shoving his gun back in its holster, he grabbed Annabelle and planted his lips on hers. For a moment her body was tense, but then she relaxed in his arms as his mouth coaxed hers into opening for him.

He melded his mouth over hers, deepening the kiss. God, this woman tempted and teased him and made him ache with a longing he'd never realized, until she'd thrust her way into his life. She reminded him of the gentler things in life. Of his home and family and he ached with longing for everything he'd lost. For the family he'd rode away from.

Right now, the Harris gang could ride up on them and catch them in the act, and he wouldn't know. She wrapped her arms around his neck, giving into the kiss completely. He pulled her tight against his groin, pushing his hardened dick into her, wanting her to know what she did to him. What had started out as a distraction for Annabelle turned into a forest fire of need for him. He drank deeply from her lips, needing to feel more of her, wanting her naked and willing in his arms.

Danger surrounded them, yet he wanted nothing more than to take her here right now on the ground.

His hand slipped down to caress the fullness of her breast through her clothes. She moaned deep in her throat, and it was all he could do not to rip the dress from her body. That sound was so enticing, so tempting, and desire pushed all rational thought from his mind. All he wanted to do was lay Annabelle on the soft ground and bury himself deep inside her—to lose himself in her soft womanly folds.

He raised her leg and wrapped it around his waist,

pushing his erection into her feminine core. Her breathing changed, and she whimpered beneath his kiss.

She shoved her hands against his chest, putting distance between them. Her breathing was harsh and jagged. "What the hell are you doing?"

She dropped her leg from around his waist and walked a short distance from him. Her chest was rising and falling rapidly, and he knew she'd been just as affected by that kiss as him. She put her hand to her mouth and touched it gingerly. Glancing out at the road, she asked, "Are you trying to get us killed?"

"No, but I thought if we were going to die, I wanted one last kiss."

A frown crossed her forehead, and she gazed out at the road like she was trying to understand. "Make certain that's your last kiss. Because there won't be anymore."

He folded his arms across his chest and stared at her. "Why?"

The longer he could keep her away from the trail, the better his chances were of surviving this rendezvous with her sisters. They had to get further down the road, where Annabelle couldn't see them.

"Seems pretty obvious. You're going to hang, and I don't want to become involved with a man whose time here on earth is short."

He chuckled. "What if I wasn't going to die?"

She turned and faced him. "You're a devilishly handsome man, but you're wanted by the law, and you're off limits. No kissing. No touching. Nothing. Stay away from me, Beau."

She whirled and started walking through the brush toward the path.

"Where are you going? We need to stay hidden," he

called after her, hurrying to catch her.

But Annabelle didn't slow down. When she reached the trail, she stared up and down. "Who were the riders, Beau? Was it the Harris gang?"

He shrugged. "Does it matter? I was too busy kissing you."

She knelt down and glanced at tracks left from the riders. When she stood, he could see the fury flashing from her eyes as she hurried to her horse. "You son of a bitch. They were my sisters. You weren't kissing me because you wanted one last kiss. You were distracting me, so I wouldn't see them."

Oh God, he was in trouble again. Nothing seemed to get past this woman. And he couldn't let her go after them. He couldn't let her yell or do anything that would attract attention. He needed her to calm down and stay with him.

"Now why would I do that? I'd just as soon turn you over to them and get you out of my hair, so I could be on my way."

"Because you knew they would have arrested you."

She opened her mouth to yell, and he covered her lips with his hand. "Now, stop and think about what you're about to do. The Harris gang is probably not far behind us, and then we'd have everyone here on top of us. There could be a shoot-out and someone could die. Is that what you want?"

She bit his finger. Not hard, but enough that he yanked his hand back. "Damn you, woman. How did you know from looking at their tracks they were your sisters?"

"See, I knew you were trying to distract me." She rubbed her mouth across her dress sleeve. "Damn

114

cheating, lying man."

"You didn't answer me. How did you know that was them from looking at the tracks?"

"Why should I tell you? You just might use it against me." She all but stomped back toward her horse. Her mouth was pinched, and in the three days they'd been together, this was the angriest he'd made her. He needed to try harder. It was one way to keep them from kissing.

"You shouldn't have stopped me from seeing them. Now I can't trust you."

He squatted down and examined the tracks in the trail. One of the horses only had five nails in the horseshoe, while the others all had eight. He couldn't have fooled her.

Walking back to where she was climbing into her saddle, he grabbed her horse's bridle and held him. "I have to get to that bank money before the Harris gang. Once we find the money and we reach Fort Worth, then I will take you to your sisters. And I'll even give you the five hundred dollar reward money."

Her eyes all but branded him with their flashing fire. "I won't be bought off. I'll earn my money the honest way. If you want to give me your money, that's your choice. But I'll still turn you in."

"I just bet you would," he said, shaking his head.

Her forehead wrinkled in a frown. "Why is it so important you reach Fort Worth?"

"I've got a sick aunt who needs the money for an operation back east," he said, unable to tell her the truth.

She shook her head. "See, this is why I can't trust you. That is an outright fib. I'd rather you told me you were going to gamble it away. Don't lie to me."

He sighed and took a deep breath. "I'm trying to

protect you. You may not understand, but I can't tell you everything without endangering you."

"Like you haven't already put me in jeopardy?"

God, she had a point, but he couldn't tell her the truth without risking her life, and he wanted to protect her. He liked this smart, sassy woman more than he should, and it was going to get him killed.

"Maybe I owe another outlaw cash, and he said, 'Get it to me before the end of the month or your sister dies'. Would you understand then?"

Once again, he was lying, but he couldn't tell her everything. Not yet. And even then, she was going to be madder than a rained-on rooster.

"You're air'n your lungs, but I'm not buying what you're saying."

He let go of her horse's bridle. "Let's go before the Harris gang shows up. I'm not ready to die just yet."

"I don't want you dead either, just yet. I've got to get paid for your bounty and the five hundred dollars cash you promised me. I'll be a rich woman, while you swing from a noose."

Beau shook his head and then crawled up on his horse. "Damn, woman, you are one stubborn miss. No matter what I do it's the wrong thing."

She looked over at him and smiled, her blue eyes twinkling. "Glad to know I'm getting under your skin. Now, you know how it feels."

"If I didn't think the Harris gang would find you and kill you, I'd leave you at the next farmhouse and go on my merry way."

"Do it," she dared him. "I'll leave and go find my sisters. We'd have you arrested before sunrise."

He couldn't win. And yet, he enjoyed watching her

try to outwit him. She was the only woman he'd ever met who could take what he gave her and give it back double. And it made him wonder how she'd respond when he made love to her.

Beau raised his eyes heavenward. "I know I'm a sinner, Lord, but please save me from this crazy woman."

Shaking her head, she laughed and rode away. "You're in so much trouble, Beau. You best be saying your prayers."

Beneath his breath, he mumbled. "I am. Lord, help me get out of this mess."

*

Two hours later, sitting on their horses hidden behind trees and bushes, they watched as the Harris gang rode down the trail. As the dust settled, Annabelle heaved a sigh of relief. "I feel better with them in front of us."

She'd feel even more relief when her sisters caught up with her. She was glad to know they were actively searching for her.

Well, she'd left them another little clue in the grass. Hopefully, they'd found her secrets pointing them where she was headed, and they'd keep looking in the right direction.

"That just means they could be waiting for us around the next bend," Beau said, his eyes watching the men's backs disappear.

"Always have to spoil it for me, don't you." Now, she wouldn't feel safe.

He grinned at her. "Well, it's the truth. We've got to remain alert until we reach Fort Worth."

"And how long will that take?" She wanted to find her sisters and go home as soon as possible. Beau Samuel was much too tempting a man. And he had a price on his head.

"At least four days. That's if I can find the bank money quickly."

"Another week with you."

"Think about how much you'll have to tell your sisters."

Patting her horse on the neck, she glanced at him. Oh, he thought telling her sisters was funny, but Annabelle knew differently.

"You have no idea what my sisters are capable of doing to you when they find you. They'll hurt you if they think you've acted improper with me."

"What if you act improper with me? Who's going to protect me?" he asked.

She shook her head at him, feeling her body tense with frustration. "Beau Samuel, it would be wise for you to tighten your smart mouth. Your mother must have had a time with you."

He shrugged then turned his horse, heading deeper into the woods away from the trail. "I was probably her easiest son to raise. Her nicest one, as well, though she never appreciated me."

Beau led them in a northwesterly direction away from the trail and the Harris gang. Hopefully, they would continue north, but there was no guarantee. She glanced around, looking for moving bushes or trees, wishing it was her sisters she would see, not the gunned wild bunch they'd just witnessed.

"How many brothers and sisters do you have?" she questioned.

"There were my two older brothers Frank and Jesse James, sisters Susan, Sarah, Fannie, and brother Archie

118

Samuel."

For a moment, Annabelle felt her heart skip a beat at the realization. Her lungs seized and she could hardly breath. "Are you telling me Jesse James is your brother?"

He laughed. "Yes, ma'am. He's my older half-brother."

"Oh, dear God," she said. "Why did you tell me? I can see why you wouldn't want the world to know you were Jesse James' brother. Why are you telling me?"

"I don't know. You're easy to talk to."

"Does the gang know?"

He glanced over at her and smiled. "It's not something I share with everyone. No, they don't know."

She shook her head. "God, I'm certainly glad I chose you to follow out of the bank. Nothing like bringing down the wrath of the James clan when you hurt one of their own."

"Yes, ma'am," he said with a laugh. "That's why I'm grateful Beauregard John Thomas Samuel is my name. I added on the Beauregard to keep people from connecting me to the Samuel family and therefore Jesse James."

She shook her head, not understanding his connection to the James gang. "If you didn't want to be recognized as a James brother, then why did you become an outlaw?"

He shrugged his shoulders like it was nothing, yet just from his actions, she knew she'd hit a nerve.

"It would be hard to be a good man and live in the shadow of your brother," she said. "In fact, I'm sure your sisters were considered renegades as well."

The movement was subtle, but she saw the way his hands clenched on the reins. "It was the hardest on our mother. She loved all her kids and still does. But when people turned against Jesse, it broke her heart."

"An outlaw family," she said.

They were only words, but Beau's stomach tightened, and his mouth turned down into a grimace. Yet, he couldn't explain why to her. If you were a member of the James or the Samuel family, you were an outlaw. A wanted man, regardless. You were guilty before you committed any crimes.

"Let's ride," he said, clicking to his horse and urging him on. There was plenty of daylight left, and he wanted to put a lot of country behind them. He'd come to Texas after leaving the family farm in Missouri, needing to put as much distance between him and his brother's reputation.

Only now, he longed to visit his mother, see his sisters, but would they accept him back into the fold after he'd left them?

Chapter Eight

With every step her horse took, Annabelle felt like a knife stabbed her tailbone. Her muscles ached from the hours in the saddle. She'd had very little rest in the last twenty-four hours. If it weren't for the fact she was getting pierced in the butt every time her horse moved, she'd go to sleep. Beau wanted to make it before dark, but she feared the sun would set before they arrived. Their bodies were tired, and the horses were showing signs of fatigue.

"Did you hear that?" Beau asked.

"Hear what?" she said, forcing herself to become more alert. She needed to help watch for signs of the Harris gang, yet she could barely keep her eyes open. "No, I didn't hear anything but the birds chirping."

He pulled his horse to a stop.

Then she heard it—the sounds of crying. "That's a baby."

A frown marred his forehead. "Maybe it's from a farm?"

"Why would a baby be outside?" she asked.

They came out of the bushes within twenty yards of a couple with two small children and a baby. The wheel of their wagon had come off, and the man was struggling to put it back on.

The couple gazed at them warily. Annabelle could see the fear in the woman's face.

"Hello? Looks like you've had some trouble." She tried to put the woman at ease.

Beau was already sliding off his saddle. He ground tethered his horse and went to help. The man was showing Beau where the pin had snapped on the wheel and how he was trying to fix it.

The outlaw was trying to help a stranger fix his family's wagon.

Every time she thought she hated Beauregard Samuel, he did something nice, either for her or someone else to make her reconsider.

Annabelle swung her leg over and slid off her horse then walked over to the woman. "Hi, I'm Annabelle, and that's my husband, Beau. We're from Zenith."

"Nice to meet you," the woman said. "I'm Irene and that's Jack, my husband."

"How old are your children?"

"They're four and two years old and the baby is six months," she said. The baby began to cry again. "Sorry, he's teething, and he's been very fussy."

"Are you from around here?" Annabelle asked.

"Yes, we live about five miles down the road. We were almost home," the woman said, glancing over at the toddlers.

They seemed like a nice family, and Annabelle felt a moment of jealousy. This was what she wanted, a family of her own with children and a loving husband— someone to talk to, besides the chickens, when her sisters were gone.

There would come a day her sisters found husbands of their own and moved away from Annabelle and the farm. She could be living alone.

There was a moment of silence, and then the woman turned to Annabelle. "How about you and your husband?"

"No babies," Annabelle responded, wanting to correct the lie she'd told this woman and tell her they weren't married. But if the Harris gang stopped them, the couple might tell the outlaws Beau and Annabelle weren't married.

"I'm so glad your husband is helping mine. I was worried he would get hurt trying to fix the wagon. It was so nice of you to stop and help us," she said, gazing over at the men who were squatted down, talking about the best way to fix the wagon.

How would the woman feel if she knew the man helping her husband was Jesse James' brother? Would she still feel grateful? Doubtful.

And though Annabelle knew Beau was an outlaw, how many men would stop and help a couple in need? Wouldn't most rob the family since they were in a dire situation? She watched as Beau lifted the wagon while the man slid the wheel back on. Then they worked together to tighten the wheel.

"Excuse me," the woman said to Annabelle. "Would you mind holding the baby, while I excuse myself for a moment? I never seem to get time to go to the bushes alone."

Annabelle chuckled. "Of course."

She held out her arms for the baby, and the woman placed him into Annabelle's arms. For a moment, she felt awkward. Years had passed since Ruby was a small child. In fact, her mother had still been alive when Ruby was a toddler. The memory of her mother and her sisters made her release a sigh. God, she missed all of them— her mother and now her sisters. Surely, they would realize they'd lost her trail and come back, but what if they ran into the Harris gang?

It was a constant worry.

The baby gazed up at her with a frown on its face.

"Hello. I should have asked your mother your name."

The child reached out and grabbed a piece of her hair.

"No. No, I still need that hair. Soon you'll have your own." She rocked the baby in her arms, swaying from side to side. For a brief moment, she imagined he was her baby, and the only person she could think of who could possibly be his father was Beau. But that was crazy.

Someday. Someday, she would have a husband and children. Someday. Her heart squeezed painfully and she sighed, longing pumping through her veins. And Beau…

Beau would hang for the crimes he'd committed. There was no future with an outlaw.

She thought of Beau's mother. Three of her sons were outlaws, men hunted by the law, who would probably die an early death. She gazed down at the child, and her heart ached for Beau's mother. Regardless of what her children had done, she still loved them. She didn't want them to die.

A moment later, the mother came back. "Oh, thank you. I needed that break. You'll learn that with toddlers and babies you never get a break."

"I'm sure that's true." Annabelle handed the baby back to his mother. "He was very good. What's his name?"

"George," she said.

"He's a cute little fella." Annabelle wished she and Beau could get going again. She didn't like lying to people, and she felt like everything she said to this woman was a lie.

The men stood up and shook hands. Annabelle could see the wheel was restored.

"Thanks for helping us," the man said to Beau.

She felt a rush of pride. The family had obviously needed assistance, and Beau had stopped and offered his help. How many outlaws would have done such a thing? But Jesse James' brother had lifted the wagon, giving the family support. People would assume he was a killer, just like his brother. Personally, she would never have believed this tale if she hadn't seen with her own eyes how he'd lent a hand to a stranded family.

"Looks like your buckboard is fixed," Annabelle said to the woman.

"Your husband was so kind to stop. I don't think Jack could have lifted that wagon without him," she said, trying to herd her children to the repaired vehicle.

What Beau had said about people suddenly made perfect sense. Would anyone believe Jesse James' brother helped a stranded family? She was Ruby McKenzie's sister, the girl expelled from school for charging boys to kiss her. Did that mean Annabelle would let a boy pay her for kisses? Absolutely not.

Yet, wouldn't most people compare Beau to Jesse and not give him a chance?

An ache began in her midsection. No wonder he'd turned to a life of crime. Not many people would give him a chance, but rather assume the worst about him.

"No problem. You might want to try to make it home tonight. There's a dangerous gang running in these parts," Beau warned them.

After loading the wagon, Jack helped his wife into the vehicle and then handed up their children to her. He turned and shook Beau's hand. "Thanks again. I appreciate it. I hope you reach Fort Worth safely."

"Thanks," Beau said.

The woman waved to Annabelle, and they drove off leaving her and Beau behind.

"Do you think we should follow them, just to make certain they reach their home okay?" Annabelle asked as their wagon bounced along the trail.

She didn't want to delay her and Beau reaching the Red River, but she also worried the Harris gang would find the family and hurt them.

"No, they're headed in the opposite direction. I think they'll be okay. They've got almost two hours left of daylight," Beau said, gazing over at Annabelle. "Let's get going."

"Yeah, we lost some time there."

"Some things can't be helped," Beau said and climbed on his horse.

"You surprise me. I'm glad we stopped and helped them."

He grinned at her. "Yeah, all outlaws have black hearts and eat small children. You wouldn't think they would stop and help someone."

She shook her head at him, frustration filling her at how she'd thought he was kind for helping that family. Why, when she began to believe he was a nice guy, did he say something that made her want to smack him? "You are such a weasel."

"I aim to please," he said and gigged his horse.

The break was over, and once again, Annabelle was

jostled in the saddle as they headed down the trail.

*

With only the moonlight guiding them they continued on down the trail until Beau knew he had to admit it was time to call it a night. When Annabelle learned they would be camping without a fire, she was going to be angry. But he wasn't taking a chance on either the smell or the sight of a campfire luring in the Harris gang. No, it wouldn't make for a comfortable night, but being dead wouldn't accomplish what he needed to do.

He pulled his horse into a grove of trees far enough off the trail that they would be hidden.

"Your hotel for the night," he said to Annabelle.

"Your choice in accommodations is lousy," she replied, swinging her leg over the saddle. "And the light is so bad it's going to be hard to find wood."

"No fire tonight." He was certain she would now begin to throw a fit because they couldn't have a fire to keep warm and keep the animals at bay. But he was worried more about two-legged animals than four.

She turned and he could feel her gaze on him, but he couldn't see her expression. "Oh."

For a moment, he was stunned. She wasn't complaining, in fact, she accepted the fact that there would be no fire for them to cook on or get warm by.

"It's going to be a chilly night."

"Yes," he replied, thinking of how he was going to feel with no bedroll to snuggle down into, only the cold hard ground beneath him.

"I'll see about opening us up a jar of peaches," she said. "Or you can have cold green beans."

He laughed. "Frankly, I'd be happy with some peaches, and there's some dried beef jerky in my saddlebags. I'll get it."

Together the two of them unsaddled their horses and tethered them to a nearby tree. Beau pulled out some oats and fed both animals. They worked side-by-side in the dark to set up their camp.

A few moments later, he joined Annabelle on the horse blankets she'd laid on the ground. She handed him a fork.

"Where did you get forks?" he asked.

"Since I had to clean the dishes back at the Harris encampment, I thought maybe they just might not need these utensils any longer. I slipped two of them into my dress pocket."

A chuckle erupted from within him at the thought of the gang sitting around the campfire to eat and someone having to use his fingers. "You stole from a band of thieves? Doesn't that make you a thief?"

"Hey, I learn from the best. Besides, it was payment for washing their dirty dishes."

They sat in the darkness, the stars shining down upon them, the glow of the moon their only light.

"Did you like being a farmer?" she asked.

He thought about his time on the farm. Until she'd brought it up, he hadn't realized how much he missed the routine—the early mornings, the seasons, the caring for their animals, and the harvests. The way his mother and even his father had helped make the hard work fun. He'd enjoyed his life until the Civil War ended. That had been the beginning of the end.

His family had owned slaves and sided with the South, believing the South would once again be resurrected. His brother Jesse had fought and even today continued to fight for the Southern cause, but Beau didn't agree.

And for that reason, he'd been ostracized by his family. Told to leave when he didn't agree to join what his brothers were fighting for.

The memories were painful. Even now, his chest ached with the knowledge he was the true rebel in the family. The one who believed both sides were wrong. And yet, people assumed he was just another outlaw in the family. Another fighter for the Southern cause.

Just like Annabelle.

"I miss the farm. I miss my family," he said, and he did. An aching sense of sadness filled him at the thought of his family, his mother. She'd suffered so much at the hands of her children. Including, losing a limb last year to the incendiary device the Pinkerton's threw into the house and the subsequent blast that killed his half-brother. All because Jesse continued the rebel fight.

The war was over. And so was Beau's connection to his family.

"Papa use to talk about the James brothers," she said. "He's probably rolling over in his grave right now with me sitting here beside you."

"Yeah, we're all a bad lot," he said sarcastically. "The Union army tortured my father, trying to learn where my half-brother Frank's group of men were. They made us abandon our farm in Clay County. My mother suffered the loss of her arm, and my youngest brother was killed. Not to mention the everyday harassment by the locals."

A fierce anger filled him. He took a deep breath, calming the pulsing hatred, while reliving the worst days of his life. "Clay County, Missouri was 'Little Dixie', and the culture was extremely pro-slavery, but there were local Unionists who hated us."

She gazed at him with what appeared to be understanding in her eyes, not contempt or aberration, but rather sympathetic perception. A sense of belonging came over him. He felt the words tumbling from his mouth that he'd never voiced to another human being, though secretly they'd known.

"I didn't believe in slavery. As a little boy, my best friend Joshiah was a slave on our farm. We'd played together as far back as I can remember, until they put him to work in the fields." Beau remembered that day like it was yesterday. "My father told me it was past time for Joshiah to earn his keep. He had to work. And he had, right up until the day Jesse killed him."

Annabelle gasped. "What happened?"

"He got caught stealing."

"That's hardly a killing offense."

"It is when you belong to an owner who believes your life means nothing," Beau said. His brother had been young. Home from the war recovering from a chest injury, Jesse had been filled with hate and distrust and fear that his way of life was ending before it had barely begun. Killing Joshiah had been a power move, one to show the Negroes that Jesse was in control. It had cost Joshiah his life and Beau his friend. It had been stupid and senseless, and Beau hated Jesse just as much today as he had back then.

An owl hooted somewhere nearby, and Annabelle shivered.

"Cold?"

"I'm not sure if I'm cold or disturbed by what you just told me. We never had slaves. Our papa didn't believe in slavery. Joshiah was your friend, your playmate. Couldn't you stop them?"

When Beau heard Joshiah was in trouble, he'd gone running to the slave quarters, but he'd arrived too late. And Jesse…his brother had seemed almost gleeful when he'd seen the pain on Beau's face. He'd called Beau despicable names for befriending a black boy.

"He was dead before I found out. It was the first time I've ever wanted to kill someone. Jesse told me Joshiah was just a blackie and asked me why was I getting myself all worked up over his killing. Then he told me I needed to grow up and become a man. I learned to hate at that moment. Hate what my brother had become."

That hate still fueled some of Beau's decisions, though lately, it seemed to have backed off some. If it hadn't been for his mother, he would have killed his brother.

Annabelle sighed. "I've been plenty mad at both of my sisters, but I've never hated one of them."

"I did. We've never been close, but I still have to live with his actions every day."

A cloud covered the moon, and for a moment, he couldn't see anything. A dark night would certainly cloak them well, but still, he kind of liked to see what was out there.

"I bet most people think everyone in your family is just like Jesse. People assume a lot about a person before getting to know them."

He put down the jar of peaches he'd been eating and glanced over at her in the darkness, wishing he could see the expression on her face. Was that understanding he heard in her voice?

"Once they learn I'm related, they believe I'm just like my brother. Some people have even run from me.

Some want me to join their rebel cause. Others become very protective of their family members and slink off quietly in the night," he said. "Even if I had obeyed the law, people will think I'm an outlaw. With Jesse's reputation, I have no chance."

The first time he'd been arrested, he'd barely been eighteen. They'd held him, hoping his brother would come break him out of jail. Finally, they realized after almost a month that no one was coming to rescue him. No one, and he was okay with that.

Finally, they'd released him.

"I guess I'm assuming a lot. But you seem different from what I've heard about your brother. Of course, much of what I've seen and read could be enhanced for those dime novels."

He laughed and realized she did understand. It was hard to know what was fact and what was fiction when it came to his two older brothers. "Yeah, I don't even know what the truth regarding Jesse is anymore. We learned a long time ago not to believe everything the newspapers said. He was seriously wounded and laid up at my uncle's when he was given credit for a robbery we know he couldn't have committed."

He sighed and lay back on the ground. "A lot of people don't connect the last name Samuel and Jesse, so as long as I stay away from Clay County, Missouri, I'm all right."

Her hand reached out and covered his. "I love my sisters, and I can't imagine them hurting me so badly and then being forced to live with their reputation every day. It must be difficult."

Warm feelings overwhelmed him at her words. Tears sprang into his eyes, and he had to blink to keep them from falling. No one ever understood. Yet, Annabelle recognized his pain, his predicament.

"As long as I don't let people know who my family is, I'm usually all right. But it's also why I don't have a lot of close friends. I have acquaintances. They know who I am, but not who I really am."

She leaned onto his arm and hugged him. "You should become a farmer. I think you'd enjoy being settled and not on the constant run to acquire more money."

"We'll see," he said. "First, I have to prove to the state they really don't want to hang me."

His fingers touched her silky hair. He wanted to put his lips over hers again, but knew that wouldn't be wise.

"I think I'm going to turn in," she said and moved over to the blankets she'd set up in the dark.

He wanted nothing more than to join her in those blankets, instead of out here in the cold with no fire to warm him. And yet, he didn't dare try to insist on lying next to her. She'd probably shoot him.

"As long as you act like a gentleman, you can share the bedroll with me tonight. It's cold and you'll sleep better. We both could use a decent night's sleep."

Beau smiled. He didn't know for certain how much sleep he would get, but he was colder than frog legs. The thought of cuddling around Annabelle's sweet body was a temptation he couldn't deny.

"I'm freezing," he said and hurried over to her. Quickly, he crawled inside the blankets and wrapped his arms around her. "Now, this is nice."

She didn't respond, and he could feel her shivers slowing. "You were chilled as well."

"Yeah, it's cold tonight. Feels like winter is

determined to return."

He took a deep breath and inhaled her essence. She smelled of peaches and a soft womanly scent that reminded him of the comfort and safety of home, not the hostile months before the Civil War or the aftermath and all the tensions and destruction.

Being with Annabelle made him realize everything he missed and how by leaving Missouri, he'd run from everything—his family, their reputation, his own demons. And lying here beside Annabelle, he wanted his life to return to normalcy.

Didn't he deserve happiness? Didn't he deserve to have a home and family, one that was not riddled with strife and anger and violence?

He shuddered at the memory of Jesse and his band of cutthroats. That was not the kind of life he wanted for himself or anyone else he hitched his wagon to.

Annabelle snuggled up against him and he sighed. This feeling of a woman wrapped in his arms, warming his body, heating his soul was something he could get used to. Not just a woman, but Annabelle.

"You're not shaking any longer," he said, his voice coming out husky and deep and filled with desire for this gorgeous woman cocooning with him.

"No," she said, her voice quivering. "I'm feeling very warm, maybe I should crawl out for a while. You know sit up and gaze at the sky."

He chuckled. "Go to sleep, Annabelle. I'll watch over you tonight, keep you warm and safe in my arms. Nothing's going to happen between the two of us that you don't want."

She sighed. "That's the bad thing…you make me crave things I know I shouldn't want."

Unable to resist any longer, he kissed the back of her neck, his mouth warm and insistent on her flesh. A shiver rippled through her.

"Things like that?" he whispered, knowing he affected her just as much as she was getting to him.

"Yeah, stop that, so we can both get some sleep."

"Kiss me, goodnight," he said against her hair.

"Oh no, I can't do that."

"Why not?"

"Because that kiss would last all night. And I'm not ready for that."

Chapter Nine

All the next day a wall of tension existed between Annabelle and Beau. They didn't have that easy teasing and bantering going between them that had been there before. In fact, he seemed more on edge than ever and the nearer they got to the Red River, the more withdrawn he became. Where once he would have regaled her with stories and ribbed her, now he answered in one-syllable answers, short and to the point, and she was just about sick of it.

They'd spent the night wrapped up in each other's arms, and she had to do everything in her power to keep from rolling over and saying, "Just get on with it and take me here and now on the cold hard ground."

She wanted him like nothing ever before, but she knew it was crazy. Making love with Beau would be taking a huge risk that could leave her heartbroken. He was wanted for a hanging offense, yet every day she liked Beau just a little more. He wasn't a cold-blooded killer like she'd imagined. In fact, he seemed the exact opposite.

And as for Jesse James being his half-brother, they couldn't be more different. Or so it seemed, but then could she really know the truth about his brother? Was he beyond a doubt a cold-blooded killer or a man whose reputation had been built on lies and half-truths?

Wind whipped up trail dirt, slinging dust at her face. She ducked her head, trying to keep as much out of her eyes as possible. Clouds were beginning to form, and it looked like they were going to have to endure yet another downpour. All day the air felt like it was dripping with steamy water. The wind seemed to hiss with heat from the sun.

"Nothing like springtime in Texas," she said, clearing the dust from her face.

"Feels like it could storm," Beau said.

The tension between them was a result of sleeping side-by-side last night and waking with his arms wrapped around her. The sensation was wonderful and frightening and aroused thoughts of what could happen between the two of them.

Behind them, in the west, she noticed the clouds were building, turning dark. The thought of riding out a thunderstorm with no shelter frightened her. She looked around the wooded area and saw no place to hide. The land had flattened out, and while trees and brush were plentiful, there was no place to get out of the weather.

"I think I'm missing that cave right about now."

Beau glanced at the skies behind them and frowned. "That's not good. That one cloud is low and heavy looking. Keep an eye out for a farm. We might need to hole up until after this storm passes."

"And if we don't find a farm?"

"Then we'll be getting wet," he said.

A resounding boom rattled the air around them, and she noticed the birds were no longer chirping. In fact, they were no longer flying and seemed to have disappeared.

The wind died down, and suddenly, the air felt still and oppressive. Almost crackly with energy.

"We need to locate a shelter," Beau said, glancing around at the sky again.

The clouds were traveling faster than they were, and Beau picked up speed. Even the horses seemed to suddenly understand a storm was coming and were anxious to get out of the weather's path.

Lightning crackled behind them, and the sky was changing colors, turning a sick green.

"Those clouds look like they could contain some hail," she said worriedly.

"Yeah, come on, let's push the horses. We need to find shelter, or we're going to get pummeled," he said.

They started to gallop across the fields, rushing to some unknown destination, hoping they could find a place to get out of the weather.

"There," Beau said and pointed to a building in the distance.

Just then the wind slammed into them, and her horse whinnied in alarm. "Come on," she said as the wind threw dirt, swirling and pulling at them from all directions.

She glanced behind her, and her heart leaped into her throat, causing her to choke on the fear that bubbled up. A funnel cloud dipped down from the sky toward the earth.

"Beau," she screamed.

He glanced behind at her, his eyes growing large. "Come on."

They spurred their horses, running them at a full

gallop, pushing as fast as they could toward the farmhouse. What couldn't have been a quarter mile away seemed to take forever. Racing across the prairie, her heart pounded with fear, her ears popped as the wind howled.

Once they reached the abandoned house, Beau flung himself off his horse and slapped it on the rump. It took off running. When Annabelle reached the house, he helped her alight and then sent her horse running.

"But our horses," she cried over the noise of the wind.

"They'll take care of themselves," he said.

The funnel was now dancing on the ground, churning and eating as it spun across the earth, racing toward them. Its tail swept across the prairie, like Mother Nature's broom, gobbling up everything the horrific winds touched.

Beau grabbed her by the hand and pulled her toward the back of the house. "Come on, let's hope they built a root cellar before they left."

They ran between the barn and the house. The tin roof groaned, struggling against the pull of the wind. Just when she thought they would have to take shelter in the house, Beau located the root cellar.

He opened the door and shoved her inside. He flung himself into the darkened underground cellar and pulled the door closed, latching it against the wind with a wooden two by four they could only hope would hold. Quickly, he lit a lantern and hung it from a hook, illuminating an old bed in the corner of the shelter

The noise grew louder and louder like the sound of a thousand trains roaring overhead and the ground beneath them trembled.

"Beau," she screamed, and he wrapped his arms around her, holding her tight against his chest.

They were going to die. The wind was going to suck them up into the funnel. Her entire body shook, her heart pounding inside her chest like she was running for her life.

"It's okay," he said and squeezed her against his chest, as the earth around them shuddered and a fine mist of dirt showered over them. The door on the cellar shook and rattled, and they stepped as far back into the cellar as they could go.

"It's going to break," she screamed. They were going to die down here in this cellar, where no one would ever know they were. Their bodies would never be found, and she would never see her sisters again. She wanted with all her heart to go back to that day in the bank and return home to the place she loved.

"No, sugar, it's okay." His hands soothed her, as he gently pushed her hair away from her face.

The noise increased, and he held onto her tightly, his mouth covered hers, his lips silencing the scream that had been ready to explode from her. He placed his hands over her ears, as he held her head in place and ravished her mouth with his lips.

Tense, she held onto his shoulders, gripping him like she never wanted to let him go. Fearful the wind would suck them out of their hiding place, she knew she would cling to him as long as she could before they were torn apart.

If she was going to die, she wanted Beau holding her when they went.

Terrified, she felt them falling. They landed on the soft bed as the sound of the wind lessened. Pulling her mouth away from his, she asked, "Is it over?"

"I think so," he said, his breathing harsh.

"I was so scared," she said, her heart beating rapidly inside her chest, her limbs quaking.

"Me too," he replied, holding onto her like she was his lifeline in a sinking ship. His lips moved over hers again, and he kissed her like it was their last as his mouth ravaged hers. She met his fervor and gripped his body close to hers.

She needed him. For the last four days, she'd depended on him, she'd aided him, and she'd fought him, but right this moment, she required him like her next breath.

For the last four days, they'd lived on the edge, running from the Harris gang, tornadoes, and this incessant need for each other. No more. She wanted him and she wanted him now.

If she was going to die on this journey, she wanted Beau before she took her last breath.

She pushed open his shirt, wanting to touch his skin, to feel his chest. Pushing the cloth out of the way, she ran her hands over the feel of his hard chest muscles. His flesh rippled beneath her touch while his lips continued their assault on her. Her breathing was labored, and an ache began between her legs.

Their lips broke apart. "God, I want you so much," he said, his hands caressing her head. "But we can't."

She pushed him to his back and rolled on top of him. "We're alive."

"Yes," he said breathlessly, wrapping his arms around her. "Annabelle."

"Stop talking and show me what it feels like to make love."

Pulling out of his arms, she rose up and unbuttoned her dress, yanked it over her head while sitting on his body. Her heart pounded, rushing blood through her veins, and she knew she was taking a risk, but she didn't care. She was alive, she was breathing, and tomorrow this could all come to an end.

"Every day spent with you could be my last," she whispered.

Rain and hail pounded on the roof of the root cellar as she stared into his emerald eyes, glassy, shining with a fire that drew her to his flame. A shudder rippled through her at the knowledge of the chances she was taking, knowing she could die at any moment and willing to accept whatever risks their joining brought.

Frantically, before she could change her mind, she pulled his shirt out of his pants. While he undid the buttons, she tugged the garment from his body. When the shirt was removed, he reached up and grabbed her head, bringing her lips to his again.

His lips conveyed a message of desire and longing and oh, sweet Jesus, want. She opened her mouth greedily, accepting his unspoken acknowledgment of passion. Her blood was flowing through her veins faster than when the tornado was spinning on top of them.

Their lips broke apart and he placed his mouth on her neck as he nibbled softly to the curve of her shoulder. "Are you sure?"

"Shut up and love me," she whispered in the glow of the lantern. Frightened and thankful to be alive, she knew for certain that at this moment, she needed Beau.

Lifting her chemise, he tugged the garment over her head, exposing her breasts.

"Oh, God," he said as he lowered his mouth to her

puckered nipple, tenderly sucking the tiny bud.

A burst of fire flooded her and she gasped, throwing her head back, arching her chest toward his mouth. The sensation flooded her with desire for this man, an outlaw with a despicable reputation and a gentle, kind soul.

His hand gripped her breast as his tongue lavished her nub, filling her with a sweet ache that seemed to radiate all the way to her toes. Then he flipped her onto her back. Rising from the bed, he quickly shucked his pants and boots.

When he stood, even in the gloom, she could see him in all his naked glory. His manhood jutted out from his body like a weapon looking for a shield.

"So that's what a naked man looks like," she said softly.

He laughed then reached down and untied her boots. They fell to the ground with a clunk as he slid her stockings down her legs. His fingers reached for her pantaloons, and she lifted her hips to help him remove the garment.

Lying naked before his eyes for a moment, she doubted her decision. His gaze traveled over her breasts, her hips and then back.

"You're beautiful just like I imagined."

She was giving herself to an outlaw, a man with a tortured past, a man with no future. Yet, she couldn't deny she wanted him worse than she wanted her next breath. She needed Beau, if only for this moment.

He crawled up on the mattress beside her, until they lay side by side, their naked skin touching. His lips covered hers once again, and the heat that had been simmering burst inside of her like an explosion of fire, sizzling her from her head to her toes.

Annabelle ached to touch him, to slid her fingertips along his skin. She reached out and trailed her fingers down his face, to his chest, feeling the hardened muscles rippling beneath her strokes. Emboldened she skimmed her fingers all the way down his waist to his shaft.

His hand wrapped her fingers around his cock, and he moved her hand up and down. She gripped his erection, touching the tip, feeling the bulbous head on the end of his shaft.

She'd never seen a man's penis before, let alone touched one. For a moment she was in awe of the power and the strength in his erection.

At the touch of his fingers between her legs, she gasped with the zing radiating from her center. She moaned as his fingers caressed her intimately, touching her like she'd never been touched, creating a need she'd never experienced before. He stroked her until she was wet with want and filled with a raging desire that had her arching against his hand.

His lips covered hers, raking the inside of her mouth with his tongue, teasing and dancing, retreating and withdrawing, while he shifted his body over the top of hers.

She knew what came next, had dreamed of being with the right man. But this man was only the right man for the moment, and she didn't know if she would live to see tomorrow. She needed Beau, and she needed him now.

He guided his penis to her entrance and then surged ahead, powerful and yet tender—and met a wall of resistance.

"You're a virgin?" he said between clenched teeth.

"Just do it," she said, not caring that he had

questioned her virginity.

Beau pushed forward, she felt the barrier give way, she cried out as pain replaced pleasure.

He paused for a moment. "Just breathe. It'll soon pass."

She reached up, needing him to continue, wanting this man to finish what he'd started. She pulled his mouth to hers, and then she moved her hips.

He groaned as he moved within her. He drove himself into her body, and she welcomed each thrust. Heat spiraled through her, building each time he plunged into her with an intensity she'd never experienced.

"Beau," she moaned. "What's happening?"

His face was tense and full of pleasure, his emerald eyes boring into hers, lifting her and carrying her with him. "Annabelle."

Outside, thunder rumbled and rain pounded on the earthen roof, and inside, she felt like a storm was building to a crest. She met his thrusts with equal force, each stroke spiraling desire higher and higher in her, pushing her toward some unknown crest.

Then she was falling, tumbling over the peak and plummeting, falling as her body tensed and shudders shook her deep to her core. Beau's mouth locked on hers as he held onto her, thrusting into her one more time as his body tensed around her.

He released her mouth and slumped down over her. "Oh, God."

She lay there panting, her body slowly recovering, amazed at what had just happened.

Rain softly hit the roof, and he rolled off her body, still holding her close. His breathing slowed, his eyes were closed, his chest rising and falling. "Why didn't you tell me you were a virgin?"

For a moment, she tensed. Did they have to have this discussion now? "Why did you think I wasn't a virgin?"

He laughed, rose up on an elbow, and gazed at her, his emerald eyes sparkling in the dim light. "Because most women aren't bounty hunters. They don't follow strange men out of town, and they most definitely do not allow men to cuddle with them in their blankets."

The warm afterglow receded as she stared up at him. "Oh, so because I'm a bounty hunter, you thought I was a loose woman? Because I went after a man with a bounty on his head and wasn't some trembling sissy woman? And because I didn't want you to freeze last night, I'm a loose woman?"

Why did people assume a strong woman was an easy woman, when in fact, it was probably the opposite?

"Maybe not loose, but you're definitely not a typical woman."

"If you wanted an ordinary woman, then you should never have considered me."

He rolled over, pinning her to the bed. "This has been building between us since that first kiss. I've tried to avoid this collision, but you were the one who wouldn't let it go. You were the one who wanted me to make love to you."

And she had wanted him fiercely. Still did. With him lying on top of her, his chest against her own, she wanted nothing more than for him to take her again.

"Well, now you did. How does it feel?"

His hand reached out and stroked her face. "It feels damn good. So damn good I think we should have a second go at it."

She glanced up at him. "Really?"

Just then, she felt him hardening against her leg. "So for a first-timer, I wasn't too bad?"

He chuckled. "Oh sugar, I don't know whether to curse that tornado or thank it. That whirlwind sent you flying into my arms."

Warmth spread through her, and she gazed up into Beau's eyes. How could a man who was so kind, so gentle, so rough and tough and fun, swing from a rope? She pushed the vision out of her mind and concentrated on the time she had in his arms.

"Do it again, Beau. Show me again what happens between a man and a woman."

"With pleasure," he said and lowered his mouth to hers.

Chapter Ten

Beau rose from the bed and pulled on his long johns then his pants. He could feel her eyes on him, watching him. They'd made love not once, but twice. While he'd enjoyed every single second, now he felt this urgent sense to walk away. To put as much distance as he could between him and Annabelle. Because if he didn't, this woman was going to wrap her tentacles around his heart and ensnare him forever.

Even now, he wanted to do nothing more than crawl back on that mattress and wrap her in his arms again. He didn't know if he could much longer resist her sweet tempting body and the way she made him feel, but he needed to try. There was no place in his life for a permanent woman or a home or kids or any of the things she longed for.

The afternoon sun was lighting the root cellar, and he glanced around at the shelter that had saved their lives. The small dank room was empty, save for the old bed they'd fallen on.

How did he handle this thing that was exploding between them? How did he tell her this didn't mean forever? That nothing had changed between them, except now they knew each other a little better?

How could he stop this ache that squeezed his chest and left it feeling hollow and empty?

"I think I'd better go outside and check on the horses. Hopefully, they didn't wander far," he said, stuffing his shirt back into his pants and slipping on his boots.

She gazed up at him, her blue eyes sparkling with tears. She knew. Damn, the woman was no fool. She could see that like a coward, he was running.

"You do that," she said, starting to rise, searching the floor for her clothes.

He handed her dress and pantaloons to her.

"You okay?" he asked tentatively, knowing the answer, but needing to make certain she was okay.

What had he done? He'd gone against all his principles and had sex with her, leaving the possibility of a baby—a child without a father.

Yet, he didn't regret one minute of laying with Annabelle. Those minutes of being in her arms were some of the most satisfying of his life.

"I'm fine," she said and pulled her chemise over her head. With a tug, the material uncovered her face, and she gazed at him, her sapphire eyes flashing. "Just because we did this doesn't mean anything has changed between us. You're still a wanted man, and I'm still a bounty hunter. You still have a five hundred dollar reward on your head."

He breathed a sigh of relief, yet a heaviness filled his chest. Things were back to normal. It didn't appear their love-making had changed her mind. She still wanted him to hang and to collect that reward money. Why did he feel disappointed? She was giving him a way out of a delicate situation, yet he was dissatisfied?

"You know, sugar, I think you're one money-hungry woman. Five minutes ago you were laying all sweet and cuddly in my arms, and now you're ready to turn me over to the sheriff."

She smirked. "You did your part. When I thought we were going to die, you showed me what could happen between a man and a woman. Now, it's back to business as usual." Turning her back to him, she pulled on her pantaloons.

There was no place in his life for a woman. She would only be a liability that he didn't need. But why did those moments in her arms feel so right, and now everything seemed so wrong?

*

Annabelle managed to keep the tears at bay, until she heard Beau slip the wooden bar back from across the door and his boots ascend the stairs.

Damn stubborn-headed man. Sure, she had known the situation between them, but still, she'd expected more. Not a confession of love, but what? Regret? Confirmation of feelings? I enjoyed taking your virginity? What?

She'd wanted something more, but as soon as he was satisfied she could feel his itchiness to run. What if they'd created a baby? What would she do?

Tears slipped down her cheeks, and for the first time in a week, she let herself cry. This adventure had not turned out like she'd expected, and right now, she just wanted to go home. She wanted to be around her sisters and gather strength from their support and love.

She needed them near, yet they still hadn't found her.

And God, she prayed they had not been near the path of that wicked tornado. One more thing for her to worry

150

about.

Dabbing at her eyes, she glanced around the root cellar and shook her head. This was a hell of a place to lose her virginity—a cold, damp cellar with a tornado whirring overhead.

And she'd all but begged the damn man to take her. The dust from the trail must be eating her brain, yet she didn't regret one minute of being with Beau. Now she had to protect her heart—for he was not the man of her dreams. He was a man without a future.

Wiping her face, she took a deep breath, stood, pulled her shoulders back, and held her head high. She was all right. She could do this. Come hell or high water, the Harris gang or a tornado, she was stronger than all of them.

Climbing the ladder, she crawled out of the root cellar and blinked in amazement. Everything was gone— the dilapidated farmhouse, the barn, the fence, everything. It appeared that Mother Nature had used the swirling winds like a broom and swept the area, taking everything in its path. Even the leaves on the trees that were left standing were stripped bare.

"Oh my," she said twirling around in a circle. "It's gone. It's all gone."

Beau looked stunned standing there, staring at the scene. "We'd be gone too if we hadn't found that cellar."

She nodded and noticed there were fallen trees in a path that headed easterly. "The horses?"

"No sight of them."

"Our food, everything?" she said with a sudden realization.

He bit his lips and gazed at her, then nodded.

It was all too much. After everything they'd endured

for the last four days, it was all just too much. Laughter bubbled up from a place she'd never known, and she shrieked hysterically.

Beau ran to her. "Are you okay?"

Doubling over chuckling, she felt his arms pulling at her. Her body tingled like ants were crawling along her spine, and her stomach clenched. She rose and stared into his worried emerald eyes. Earlier they had gazed at her with such passion and something she'd imagined was love. Now, they stared at her looking for signs of craziness.

And maybe she was losing it—but it wasn't his concern.

"I'm sorry, but we've been running, trying to stay alive and stay hidden from the Harris gang, and Mother Nature just took our defenses away. We're going to have to walk to the next town. We have no choice," she said, laughing again.

Beau hung his head. "Yeah, I know. And we're losing daylight. We better leave, so we can get down the road a ways before nightfall."

The ground was muddy and puddles were everywhere. When the sun went down, it would be cold, dark and damp.

"Oh, yeah, another night on the trail, and this time we don't even have a bedroll to share. This time we don't have a flint to start a fire," she said, her voice rising in agitation.

He pulled her into his arms and wrapped them around her, soothing her. "It's okay. We outran a tornado. We've survived the Harris gang. A little walk won't hurt us."

She pulled back and gazed up at him. "I think the dust is eating your brains too."

Stepping out of his arms, she realized she needed to put up a defense against this man who had claimed her body, her soul, and was aiming for her heart. "Time's a wasting. Let's get going."

He smiled. "Buttercup, I knew I could count on you to see the bright side of our troubles."

If she'd been feeling any amount of warmth toward him, he'd just killed that emotion like he'd taken a gun and shot her. "Call me *buttercup* one more time, and you'll be seeing something bright all right. Now, let's get a move on before it gets too dark to see."

"Yes, ma'am," he said with a smile.

*

They had walked for what seemed like days, but Beau knew it was probably only a couple of hours. The sun was beginning to descend in the sky, and he knew the coming night would be long and cold and miserable.

"Beau, there's a single rider and it looks like… Oh God, he has our horses."

She started running toward the man before he could stop her. "Annabelle, stop."

What if it was a member of the Harris gang or worse? He watched her, hair flying, skirt raised, her legs scrambling to reach the man.

She never heard him, and he had to run to catch her.

"Stop," she called as she ran toward the man.

It was then that Beau saw the man fully. The sun bounced off the badge on his chest. Oh God, just what he didn't need. A run in with a lawman.

The man pulled to a stop. "Hello, what's wrong?"

"You have our horses," she said, running up to him, breathing hard.

He looked over at Beau then down at Annabelle.

Beau felt his nerves tingling with alarm. What if Annabelle turned him in? Did she want the bounty enough to take him to jail after they'd had sex or did she just want to be rid of him?

If the lawman recognized Beau, he could cause trouble. He'd try to take him in, and Beau wasn't leaving Annabelle. Not until she turned him in.

"I found these two feeding along the trail," he said. "How do I know they're yours?"

"Let go of the reins," she told him. The man let go and Annabelle whistled. Her horse trotted over to her and nuzzled her with its nose.

The sheriff nodded. "Yes, I'd say he was yours."

Beau joined the group. "Hello," he said, trying to catch his breath. He walked over to the man and shook his hand. "Beau Samuel. I see you found our horses."

"Yes, your wife just showed me they're yours."

Beau glanced suspiciously over at Annabelle. Here was her opportunity to turn him in. He tried to act normal, but his heart was racing like a wild mustang sprinting across the prairie. This was her opportunity to garner her reward.

"Yeah, we were in the path of a tornado, and I let the horses go, hoping they'd outrun the twister."

The man nodded. "That was a bad storm. When I found them, they were grazing. I figured with the saddles, someone was missing their horses."

"Where are you headed?" Beau asked, thinking maybe he could convince Annabelle to ride off with the man, and he could continue on without risking her life anymore. If she didn't turn him in first. So far she was keeping her mouth shut, and he hoped that would continue, at least until she was safely headed down the trail with the sheriff.

After this afternoon, the sooner he and Annabelle parted company the better. Before they got even more tangled up together than they already were.

"I'm headed to Zenith," he said. "I need to speak to the sheriff on official business."

Annabelle's head jerked up, and she stared at Beau.

"Would you mind letting my wife ride with you? She has family there and knows the sheriff," he said. "She could probably help you find your way around town."

"No," Annabelle said, her voice firm and her blue eyes flashing. "I'm not leaving you behind, sugar. We need to get to your mother and take care of her." She turned and glanced at the lawman. "His mother is on her deathbed. So, you finding our horses is such a neighborly thing to do. Thanks so much."

She put her leg in the stirrups of her horse and climbed on the animal's back. She looked at Beau, giving him a purposeful stare. "Nice meeting you, Sheriff. You ready, buttercup."

The woman was a piece of work. She'd out and out lied to the lawman about him having an ailing mother, and she was outright sarcastic when she called him sugar and buttercup.

Well, two could play this game if that's what she wanted. But still, he had to tread carefully or find himself facing down a lawman.

"Thanks for locating our horses and good luck on your trip to Zenith. Be careful, as there's a gang of nasty thieves on the road between here and town. Hopefully, you won't meet up with them," Beau said.

"Thanks and I hope your mother gets better." The lawman tipped his hat, spurred his horse, and rode off down the trail.

Beau watched the man disappear and couldn't decide if he was relieved or furious with Annabelle for rejecting the chance to reach safety—the opportunity for her to return to her normal life and for him to get to the bank money before the Harris gang.

For a moment, he hung his head and tried to control the anger suddenly engulfing him. He clenched his fists, wanting so badly to hit something. This day had been a series of highs and lows, and he was just about at his wit's end as to how to deal with this woman. She'd crawled under his skin and yanked and tugged on him, leaving him fit to be tied. One moment he wanted to kiss her, and the next he wanted to shoot her. Right now, he wanted to shoot her.

"Why didn't you go with that man? You could be safely home in Zenith, instead of being chased by the Harris gang," he said, walking toward her, his steps quick and sure.

He reached her horse and immediately knew he'd made a serious blunder, when he had to glare up at her.

She raised her brows at him and stared at him haughtily. "And lose five hundred dollars bounty? And the five hundred dollars you're going to pay me? Not happening. After I've gone through all this, I'm not backing away now. Escaping a band of cutthroats, a tornado, giving away my virginity in a root cellar. No way am I abandoning that bounty."

Beau thought he was going to explode right there in front of her. "Wait just a minute. Let's back up to that last statement. You were the one who kept saying, 'Show me, Beau. Make love to me.' I just did what you asked."

"Hrmph. So you did. I thought we were going to die,"

she said, her back straight, that haughty look on her face that he just wanted to kiss away until she softened in his arms.

"It was your choice. I only fulfilled your request," he said, a little more gently, though he was still mad enough to eat a hornet.

"A woman has dreams, and well…her first time should be someplace special."

"Sugar, you instigated us having sex. Don't blame me for your choice of location."

"I can blame you all I want."

"You're totally irrational."

"I can be irrational. I can be mean. I can be whatever I want to be because gosh darn it, Beau Samuel, you're not the man I was supposed to be with the first time."

Now, he understood. She was regretting bedding down with him. She regretted spending that time in his arms. Well, too damn bad. It was done.

"Again, sugar, you made the decision for us to fornicate."

"You didn't have to accept."

Beau lost it, his voice rising higher than he intended. "Damn, woman. I'm a man. What did you expect? Me to say, no thank you. Your pretty face and sweet body have been a temptation this entire trip, but I think I'll pass?" he said, exasperation making his body tense, his voice rising. "Not hardly. Frankly, it was the best damn sex of my life, and I was afraid that afterward you were going to expect a ring and a visit to the preacher man."

Damn, he hadn't meant to admit to her it was the best sex he'd ever experienced. He hadn't meant to reveal she was a temptation that was driving him crazy, but he didn't regret one minute of the time he'd spent in her arms. And frankly, he thought they were going to die as well.

"You're going to hang. Why would I marry a man who is going to die? Not happening, sugar."

An ache the size of Texas gripped his heart. There it was in a nutshell. She didn't want to marry him because she thought he was going to hang. He was a member of the most hated family in America. And she wanted a good man. He'd never be good enough for Annabelle. Never.

Chapter Eleven

Beau had that uneasy feeling. Late the next day, he sat on his horse on a bluff overlooking the Red River, searching the area. Maybe because he was so close to picking up the bank bag and heading to Fort Worth, or maybe because since they had sex, Annabelle had been withdrawn, quiet as a mouse, and moodier than a cat in heat. Or maybe it was a combination of all three, but he felt as jumpy as a bit-up old bull in fly time.

He looked for any signs of the Harris gang. All was quiet. Even the birds no longer chirped, and the only sound was the wind blowing through the trees and the faint gurgle of the river as it flowed.

A hawk swooped down, flying low over the water before landing in a tree near the river. The bank money was two big rocks over from the tree where the bird sat perched. All he needed to do was get down there, find the money, and ride as hard and fast as they could to Fort Worth.

"I'm going down there alone. You wait here for me."

"Why should I?" she asked, that strident tone back in her voice. That one that had been there since yesterday, since they'd made love with a tornado whirring above them.

"Because I need you to keep watch. If you see the Harris gang, I want you to drop rocks down the hillside. Do not take them on and do not fire a gunshot. That would only alert them to your location," he said, pushing his hat back from his eyes, giving her his sternest look. She had to obey him or risk both of their lives.

If anyone was going to die, it was him, not her.

She tightened her mouth. "I know you don't think I know how to shoot, but I can drill a can from fifty yards. I'm a great shot."

"I know, you've told me," he said. "But a can and a man are two different things."

Shooting a man was difficult and never something he enjoyed. He didn't want her to have to deal with the fact she'd put a bullet in someone.

"I can do it."

"It's not a matter of how great a shot you are, but the fact that I don't want you to die. We're doing this my way," he said trying to get her to listen to reason, feeling like he was wasting his breath.

"Oh, that's always worked out," she said with a snort.

He shook his head. "Listen carefully to me. If I get captured, you are to ride away and leave me with them."

She didn't say a word. He took her chin gently in his hand. "Do you understand?"

"Yes." She frowned. "But I don't like it. I'm just supposed to ride off and let them kill you? Not happening."

If the Harris gang were laying in wait for him, they'd kill him, and Beau couldn't take a chance with Annabelle's life. He'd die trying to protect her from these cold-blooded killers.

"Yes, it is. If they catch you, we're both dead. If they catch me, I'm dead. So you leave me to die and ride away."

"Shut up, Beau. It's not happening that way. It's just not," she said, a worried look on her face. "You're not going to get caught. You just can't."

He tried to give her a teasing smile, but he felt tense and he worried she wouldn't obey him. "Yeah, I know you need your bounty money."

"That's right. And you owe me money."

"Good Lord, woman, if I didn't have bounty money attached to me, I wouldn't be worth two hoots and a holler to you."

"You said it, not me," she said, frowning as she rested her hands on the saddle horn.

He reached into his saddlebags and pulled out her six-shooter—the gun he'd taken away from her that very first day. "I'm giving you your pistol back. Just don't shoot me in the back."

"If I'd wanted to shoot you in the back, you'd already be dead."

With a sigh, he glanced back down at the gently rolling river. "I know. That's why I'm giving you your gun back."

She reached out and took it, spun the cylinder checking for bullets, then turned her sapphire eyes on him. "Thank you."

She did seem familiar with the gun, but that didn't mean she could shoot. And he wasn't taking any chances.

With one last glance, he examined the scene, checking the river again. "I'll meet you back here in this same spot just as soon as I retrieve the hold-up money." It shouldn't take him long if there were no trouble.

"And just what are you going to do with that money?"

"None of your business," he responded.

"I hope you locate it. And I hope the law hangs you for it."

He was just about to gig his horse and head down the embankment, when her words hit him like a slap in the face. Gosh, darn it, the woman had crawled up under his skin and was tormenting him worse than a bevy of chigger bites.

Without thinking, he reached out and pulled her toward him. Sitting on their horses, he pulled her sideways in her saddle and covered her mouth with his. He'd wanted to kiss her since they'd left that root cellar. He'd wanted to brand her mouth as his own. He'd wanted to get up under her skin and torment her just like she pestered him.

He melded his lips to hers, teasing and taunting her with his tongue inside her mouth. His hand gripped her head, refusing to let her pull away and put any distance between them. God, this woman had his head and his heart all twisted up and tied together, aching with want and longing. Things a man like him had no business craving.

When her horse shook his head, he released her and she jerked away.

"What the hell did you do that for?" she asked.

He smiled. "Sugar, I wanted one last kiss just in case I don't make it back."

"You damn well better come back. You're not leaving me here in the wilderness by myself, with a dangerous gang searching for us. You owe me."

Chuckling, he gigged his horse and started down the

embankment toward the money and the restitution he sought.

Slowly and carefully, he made his way toward the water. He'd covered the bank's money with rocks then placed dead brush in front of the rocks. He could see the dead brush, and he let his horse make his way down the steep hill to the water.

That eerie tingling feeling was zipping along his spine, and he tried to ignore the warning, hoping it was nothing more than nerves. He scanned the area, looking for any signs of movement, hoping he'd be able to get the money and leave the area without any problems.

When he reached the brush, he glanced around one more time, looking to make sure he was alone. He gazed back up the embankment, trying to see Annabelle, but she was carefully hidden by the trees.

Premonition made him cautious.

He rode his horse further down the bank over to an area away from the hidden money. He dismounted and stood once again looking around. Nothing moved, except the meandering river flowing southward, the water's gentle gurgle peaceful and soothing.

Acting like he was searching, he moved the brush on the bank, kicking at rocks and pushing leaves aside. The sound of a gun hammer being pulled back had him tensing.

Damn! His premonition had been right.

"Beau, you looking for our money," William said, coming out from behind a large boulder, where he'd been hiding. Tom popped up from behind a bush, and then another man showed himself. Soon, three members of the gang were standing there in front of him; their pistols trained on him.

This couldn't be good. Not for him and not for Annabelle if she didn't do what he'd told her to do. And when had the woman ever done what he asked.

"William, good to see you," he said cheerfully.

"Liar. Where's the money?" William asked.

"How did you know where to find me?"

"Tom said it had to be near the bridge. We split up, and we're camped out half a mile from the bridge on either side. When we heard you coming down the bank, we hid. Where's the money?"

Beau shrugged. "I was hunting for it when you came up. So far, I haven't found it."

"Where's that sweet little wife of yours?" Tom asked. "She was mighty pretty, and I'm feeling a hankering for a woman. Especially after she knocked me out. She owes me."

Beau felt his insides harden as fear pumped through his veins. They couldn't find Annabelle. He'd die trying to protect her, but he was badly out numbered.

"She left me right after the tornado," Beau said with a smile. "I guess her idea of married life and mine didn't agree."

The men snickered.

God, he hoped and prayed she'd seen the Harris gang and was even now riding away. Though, knowing that stubborn woman, he suspected she was doing just the opposite.

"That was a real bad storm," William said, "but why would she leave you over a tornado?"

Beau shrugged. "Said she was tired of camping and living on the run. She was going home to her papa. Women. Can't live with them." He hoped his acting abilities were better than average, and he could convince them Annabelle was gone.

William backhanded Beau across the face, his blow stinging and shocking. "Liar."

Beau rubbed his jaw. "Now that wasn't neighborly. And over a woman."

"Fuck the woman. I'd shoot you right now if you had that money."

His heart hammered wildly in his chest because he knew for a fact William was quite capable of cold-blooded killing. Beau had to remain calm and try to appear unafraid.

"Why? Because I left you without your horses? Weren't you planning on killing me just as soon as we reached the Red River? You've not held up your part of the bargain. Why should I?"

The wind blew through the trees, and Beau hoped like hell Annabelle was riding away, leaving him. He didn't think she would, but he didn't want them to find her. She should just ride off and leave him to die.

William laughed, and Beau felt a prickly sensation like spiders crawling along his spine. He was in trouble, and for once in his life, he wasn't certain he could get out of this predicament.

"Where's the money?" William asked.

"I don't know. Maybe someone found it. I was looking for it, and either I can't remember where I put it, or it's gone."

"You're lying. You're going to die, so you might as well tell me where the money is hidden."

Beau felt one of the other outlaws come up and take his pistol away from him. Then his arms were pulled back behind him, and they tied his wrists together.

He shrugged. "I don't know."

William stared at him with the coldest, meanest eyes Beau had ever seen. Even his brothers' gazes held more warmth than this gunslinger's. The memory of him killing his own gang member several days ago flashed through Beau's memory, making him cold. Sweat beaded up on his forehead, but it wasn't from the heat.

That would be his fate once they located the gold.

"Tom build a fire and then ride out and collect the others. We're going to have us a party tonight to celebrate us finding the gold. Because by the time I'm finished with Beau, he'll be talking. He'll be singing so loudly everyone will know where the money's hidden and the location of his sweet wife."

A chill spread through Beau. The man was crazy.

"My wife has gone home to Zenith."

God, he should have returned Annabelle to Zenith before he'd gone after the Harris gang. There were so many things he regretted, and he feared he would never have a chance to make things right.

William laughed. "We'll see."

The sun was beginning to set, and Beau just hoped and prayed Annabelle had had the good sense to ride away, once she saw they had him or he hadn't return. He didn't need her trying to rescue him. He was dead. And he knew, before the night was over, he'd be praying for God to end his life quickly.

*

Annabelle was spitting mad at that crazy Beau. He'd ridden right into their trap, and from watching above, she could tell that was exactly what it had been, a snare. They'd been waiting for him. Sure, they had known the general vicinity the money was hidden in, but how had they been able to pinpoint the location so well?

Still, for him to go down there, knowing there was a chance they were waiting on him, infuriated her. When they were out of this mess, she was going to show him her displeasure.

Why were men so confident, so sure they could conquer the world and then were surprised when they got into trouble? She'd seen it with her father, Meg's lover Zach, and now with Beau.

Darkness had fallen as she watched the outlaws sitting around their campfire eating supper. Her stomach rumbled, and she longed to eat a good meal—a sit down at a table meal, where she wasn't worried about getting killed.

Beau sat with the gang, but they'd tied his wrists and legs together. He was trussed up worse than a Thanksgiving turkey.

She checked her weapon one more time and felt to make sure she had her extra bullets in her pocket. Her horse was on top of the ridge, hidden in some trees, waiting on her.

Why hadn't they killed Beau? He must not have given them the money to still be alive. Which meant that any moment now William was going to start torturing him. She knew he would. She'd overheard that promise several nights ago, and she couldn't stomach the thought.

Inching down the embankment, she had to get closer to the five outlaws. She needed to be within thirty to forty yards for her shots to be accurate. These shots had to happen quickly, or they could kill Beau before she was finished. And she had to be precise with every shot.

When she was within range, she waited to see what would happen, looking for the best opportunity to take them out one by one.

Finally, William stood. He had been whittling on a stick, making a pointed end on it, while the other men finished their dinner. Now, he placed the stick in the fire.

A chill trickled down Annabelle's spine. She didn't feel good about that stick and it being in the fire. She checked her gun one more time.

William walked to where Beau was sitting. "Where's the money, Beau?"

She watched as Beau took a deep breath. "I don't know."

William doubled up his fist and struck Beau in the face, knocking him over. One of the men sat Beau back up and pulled the stick out of the fire. The tip was glowing bright red.

"We'll start slowly. But if you don't tell me where the money is, this stick is going in your eye."

Annabelle felt her heart pounding in her chest. Before she could pull out her gun, William stuck the stick in Beau's arm. She watched him struggle against his ropes.

She couldn't watch. She couldn't take this anymore. She knew what William was going to do with that stick, and she couldn't watch him hurt Beau.

Lifting her six-shooter, she took aim and fired. The man sitting next to Beau tumbled over. She fired again and another man went down. The rest of them were running, scattering. Three more to go.

William grabbed Beau and shielded himself behind Beau's body. She should have killed him first.

A rifle fired toward her, its muzzle flashing fire in the night. She aimed her gun and heard a muffled cry as the third man went down. The bushes rustled near her.

"I'm going to kill him if you don't come out," William cried.

Gosh, darn it, but she should have killed William first.

A man jumped out of the bushes and charged her. She shot him. Four down, one to go. But William had Beau.

"Get your ass down here now, or he's dead," William screamed.

"No," Beau yelled back. "Run."

She stood. She couldn't let him shoot Beau. She had to go down there. She pulled out her petticoat pistol and tucked it in the back of the waistband of her skirt.

"Come out with your hands up now. If you're not here on the count of four, he's dead."

Crap. Slowly, she made her way down the hill. He couldn't see her, and she watched him staring into the darkness. This could work to her advantage.

As she stepped out into the glow of the fire, he stared at her.

"Where's the shooter?" he asked, lowering his gun.

She laughed out loud. Why were men so stupid? He didn't believe she had shot his gang. Well, she would make a believer of him.

"I'm the shooter," she said and whipped the gun out from behind her, putting a bullet in his forehead before he had a chance to pull the trigger on Beau. William's body slumped to the ground, and Beau stood, staring at her in disbelief.

"Damn, woman, you don't know how to obey!" Beau said, his face red with rage. "Didn't I tell you to ride off if they captured me?"

She turned and started to walk away.

"Hey, where are you going? Untie me."

"Why should I, you ungrateful snot? I'm going for

the horses, and then I'm taking you and all these dead outlaws in."

"Untie me."

"No. You're my prisoner."

"Like hell."

She turned and glanced back at him. "You didn't appreciate me saving you."

Hurt filled her as she watched him take a deep breath.

"I'm sorry, Annabelle. But good Lord, woman, you scare me. Do you know how frightened I was for you when you came out of the darkness? I was so scared he was going to put a bullet in you. I couldn't have lived with the knowledge that I'd caused your death."

For a moment, she let his words wash over her. They were nice and they left her feeling warm. "Do you believe I can shoot a gun?"

He laughed. "Sugar, yes, you definitely have a way with a pistol. Remind me not to get in a shooting match with you."

She smiled. "That's better. You wait here. I'll be back."

She walked away from the campfire and hurried toward her horse. No, she wouldn't leave him tied up, but it would do him good to be left alone, unable to do anything until she returned and cut him loose.

Let him stew for a little while and think about how she'd just saved his ornery hide.

Chapter Twelve

Beau sat back down on the hard cold ground, waiting for Annabelle to return, hoping she would. Okay, he'd handled that like a jackass, but he'd been so frightened for her safety he'd been unable to breathe. Even now his heart was racing like a jackrabbit being chased by a wolf. And that's what he'd been, the jackrabbit about to be served up to those cold-blooded thugs, until Annabelle had picked them off one by one.

She hadn't missed a shot, and when she'd come out of the darkness, her hands by her sides without a gun, he'd thought for sure they were both goners. He'd thought they were both going to be pushing up bluebonnets. But once again, this woman who astounded him, who intrigued him, had shown him her tough side.

He couldn't remember if he'd ever seen a faster shooter. She could draw quicker than a man could spit and say howdy, shooting William right between the eyes. Better than any gunfighter he'd ever seen.

A woman. His Annabelle.

Well, she wasn't his, though, damn it, she'd be a great woman to have by his side. She was soft as a cloud on the outside and tough as nails on the inside, and she smelled like pure heaven.

And her kisses could send him to the moon and back. They packed a kick better than alcohol and were mighty tasty.

She walked back into the glow of the campfire, pulling her horse behind her. After she'd tied the animal, she strolled over to Beau and gazed at him, her sapphire eyes flashing with anger.

God, he'd screwed up badly. And now he had to eat crow, unless he wanted to remain tied up. "Look, I'm sorry. Thank you for what you did. I appreciate it, and I'm sorry I didn't say it any better. But I was so afraid for you. The thought of one of them killing or hurting you scared me worse than a green bronco in a thunderstorm. You're a damn fine shot."

She smiled. "That's fancy talk for a man with a rope around his feet and ankles."

"I was only trying to protect you."

Couldn't she understand that he couldn't live with himself if he caused her death? And he'd been so frightened. He'd accepted that he was going to die, but not Annabelle.

"I can take care of myself," she said, standing defiantly before him. "Turn around, I'll untie you."

"Thanks."

"Where did you learn to shoot like that?"

"My father gave us lessons, but mainly it was just practice. I'd come home from the restaurant and practice aiming at tin cans that I drew characters on to look like my customers. Let's just say the worst customers were always on the fence, being gunned down."

Her knife cut through the knots. He shook out his hands, letting the blood rush back in. He'd thought he was going to die with those ropes around his wrist. He'd thought his life was over.

"Like I said, I'm accurate up to about fifty yards."

With a yank, he pulled out his own knife and cut through the ropes binding his legs. He hated being tied up. He hated the feeling of helplessness that there was nothing he could do.

"Why didn't you leave me?" he asked. "That's what I told you to do."

"And I told you I couldn't. Could you have gone off and left me?" she asked.

"You know I wouldn't."

Standing, the blood flowed back into his legs and feet. He started to walk and for just a second had no feeling in his left foot. Annabelle caught him with her hands and steadied him.

God, this woman had saved his butt once again.

He grabbed her and planted his lips over hers. His mouth plundered hers, greedily consuming her, drinking from her, needing her like his next breath. He sampled her mouth, sweeping his tongue across her full bottom lip.

His hands grabbed her face, slanting her mouth for a deeper exploration. One hand tangled in her hair, bringing her closer, needing her even more.

How could he live with himself if she'd died protecting him?

He kissed her hard, his mouth pummeling hers. His lips moving over hers, like he was starving. He pulled her body firm against his own, needing her close, needing to feel her heart beating beneath his.

Why this woman? Why this woman had crawled beneath his skin and tangled with his heart was

173

something he couldn't answer. He wasn't good for her. He wasn't good enough for her, and she deserved so much more than a cowboy with a well-known lawless family.

She wrapped her arms around his neck, urging him closer, holding on while his lips drank from her mouth. He imbibed from her greedily, consuming her with a pleasure he had long denied himself. Her hands urged him on, pulling him tighter as she moaned deep in her throat.

Suddenly, she went stiff beneath him and shoved him away with all her might. "No," she gasped, stepping out of his arms. "No."

He took a deep steadying breath and released it slowly, while running his through his hair, watching her. She was touching her lips, staring at him, like a trapped animal.

"No," she repeated. "We can't."

He nodded. "It's just…if you…had gone off like I told you, I'd be dead. Thank you for not listening to me."

Taking another step back, her chest rose and fell, her breathing harsh as she stared at him, her sapphire eyes radiating heat and need. "You're welcome."

"And," he said, releasing a deep breath, "I won't ever doubt your skills with a gun again."

She smiled. "Thanks."

"I don't know about you, but I'm starving. After all that excitement, I think we should eat." They needed something to occupy themselves with or else he would find his lips on hers once again.

She glanced around at the dead men lying on the edge of the campfire, where she'd shot them. "If you don't mind, could we get rid of these bodies? They're kind of making me feel a little nauseous."

He chuckled. "Sure."

While he dragged the bodies into the darkness, she took out their meager supplies and rummaged through what the outlaws no longer needed. Soon, she had a nice meal going over the warm fire.

When Beau came back, he washed his hands in the river then walked into the glow of the firelight. "That smells delicious."

"It's beef jerky stew."

"You're spoiling me. When we reach Fort Worth, I'm not going to have you to cook for me any longer."

There was nothing to stop them from reaching Fort Worth. Nothing to keep her from turning him in and putting him in jail. Nothing.

She took a deep breath and released it slowly. Why did she feel like he was the only man who had ever really understood her? Why with Beau did she feel at ease sitting around the campfire? And after today, he appreciated the fact she could handle a gun just as well as a man.

She'd never felt so comfortable with another human being, not even her sisters, like she did with Beau and that tore her up inside. He walked on the wrong side of the law. There was no way they could be together, and he'd shown no signs of wanting her, other than sexually.

With a sigh, she steeled her heart against the feelings she could feel flowing through her. The memory of William standing over Beau with that blazing hot stick in his hand and her fearing he would poke out his eyes or something drastic squeezed her heart.

Fear gripped her insides and twisted them. She couldn't fall in love with this man. She just couldn't.

She'd never been in love, never had a boyfriend, never been kissed until Beau. And now she was frightened of her feelings.

This man understood her, respected her, and was even starting to believe she was a capable woman who could take care of herself. But she could also be soft and vulnerable with Beau, and she'd never been able to be that way before.

He made her feel like a cherished woman, and that's what scared her more than anything. All her childhood dreams of a husband and children, he evoked and rekindled. Dreams she had since given up. At twenty, she was considered an old maid.

Beau stood and walked down to the river, where he rinsed his dinner plate. "That was a great dinner."

"Thanks," she said.

"You're spoiling me. Once we reach Fort Worth, I'll have a hard time adjusting back to the trail food I'm used to eating."

She smiled. "But you'll be eating jail food."

He frowned for a moment and stared at her. "What if you didn't turn me in and collect that bounty?"

"Then all of this would have been for naught. My sisters will still have to be out on the trail chasing bounties. I don't want that," she said quietly.

If it weren't for Meg and Ruby, she would leave Beau here on the trail and return home. But she had to think about them. She didn't want the burden of the farm keeping them out searching for outlaws. She'd seen how dangerous the job of bounty hunter could be and knew eventually, they could get hurt. They'd been lucky so far, but their father had died chasing a bad man and they could too.

"Your family seems close," he said.

"We are," she responded.

He stared into the fire like he wanted to throw daggers at the flames. "We were at one time, but not anymore. Frank and Jesse changed all that."

"I can't help but think about your mother. All of her sons have gotten in trouble with the law. Don't you think she wonders what she did wrong?"

"No. My mother thought Frank and Jesse were heroes. And that Archie gave his life to support their cause. Me, she's never been very proud of me."

"Why? You're doing what your brothers have done? Isn't that what she's proud of them for?"

He laughed and poked the fire with a stick he'd picked up, sending sparks flying heavenward. "No, I'm not robbing banks owned by northern industrialists, and I'm not helping continue the fight for the Southern cause. I'm just the kid who stood up to his brother for shooting a blackie. I'm the son who didn't join in with his brothers to fight for the South. I'm the black sheep of the family. I'm my mother's biggest disappointment."

How could Beau be considered the black sheep of the family? If his mother wanted her sons to rob banks and commit crimes, he was fulfilling her every wish. He had a price on his head just like his brother Jesse and Frank. What more did she want?

She shook her head. "None of this makes sense to me. If you were a lawman, then I could see why you would be on the outside of the family, but you're still robbing banks and doing wrong. If I were your mother, I'd be mad at the whole lot of you for going against the law and risking your lives for a cause that is not going to succeed. We've already seen that."

Beau reached over and touched her hand. "You have such a fiery spirit. It's one of the things I like about you."

"Yeah, well, it gets me in trouble with my family. My sisters get frustrated with me because I tell them what I think, especially when I don't agree with them. I wouldn't be here if they had agreed. But no, Meg wanted to stop bounty hunting, and Ruby wanted to continue. I wanted to go with Ruby, and Meg said no. It's a dangerous job for a woman, and I want my sisters to stop."

Beau nodded. "Bounty hunting is a perilous profession, especially for a woman."

"But if Ruby is going to continue hunting, I don't want her to go alone. And I don't want to go with her."

"You just want to get married and have a few kids. Sounds nice and normal."

She swallowed and blinked her eyes. What could she say? She wanted him, but knew he was off limits. She couldn't even think about it because it hurt way too much. "My dreams are simple."

"That doesn't make them bad. It's okay to have simple dreams. Actually, they sound really nice."

She stood and emptied the rest of her coffee into the fire. "Yeah, well, they're not going to happen anytime soon."

"You don't know that."

Oh yes, she did. God, now when she thought of a man, she would always compare him to Beau. "I know I'm out here with you, not at home. And I haven't met a man in Zenith I would even consider for a husband. Not one."

"Understand."

Silence stretched between them, and for a moment,

Annabelle thought she'd confessed too much. There was an attraction between them she'd never experienced with any other man, yet it was impossible. Beau was from a lawless family that would never allow them to have the kind of life she wanted. The law wanted him, and she had to turn him into the sheriff to get her sisters out of the bounty hunter way of life.

The two of them together was impossible.

"We better turn in. We still have two days of riding before we reach Fort Worth."

"There should be an extra bedroll now for you to sleep in."

She wanted him next to her. She didn't want him next to her. What the hell had she gotten herself into? She wanted this man so desperately, but she knew he was off limits. She had to turn him into the law. She had to, to protect her sisters. Her mind was whirling like that twister, churning with so many mixed feelings.

"I'm not sleeping with fleas," he said. "These men weren't the best bathers, and their bedrolls are probably filled with either bed bugs or fleas. If you want to sleep in one, then you can, but me, I'm crawling in with you."

A spiral of warmth went through Annabelle at the thought of his strong, warm body next to hers. How could she tell him no, when it was his bedroll, and she didn't blame him one bit for not sleeping in one of the outlaws' blankets.

And she liked him sleeping beside her. But they were alone, with no one around to chaperone them, and temptation curled inside her like a coiled snake, ready to strike.

Yet, she enjoyed the feel of Beau snug against her at night. He was warm and safe, and the man lit a fire in her she'd never felt before. She wanted him beside her.

She watched as Beau unfurled the bedroll. He arranged the blankets then glanced over at her, his eyes dark with some hidden emotion that had her blood heating. She licked her lips and tried to think of any way she could keep the distance between them.

He walked over to the fire and kicked some logs over, then glanced at her. "Come to bed, Annabelle. I want to hold you in my arms."

Oh God, how did she get away from being snug in his embrace and did she want to?

No, she wanted him.

She took two steps to the bedroll and dropped to her knees to lie down. Maybe it was wrong, but she didn't care. She wanted Beau for the time they had left together.

Chapter Thirteen

The next morning, Annabelle rode beside Beau. The night before, the moment her head hit the ground and Beau had wrapped his arms around her, she'd fallen into a deep, restful sleep. For the first time in days, she'd slept soundly, not worrying about waking to a gun in her face or the two of them being shot while they slept.

She'd dreamed of home and the farm—of her sisters playing together as little girls, while their papa had plowed the field. Even her mother had been there, and Annabelle had woken this morning feeling like her dreams were reminding her of the love waiting for her at home.

Even though her mother and father were gone, her sisters would welcome her back in their loving arms and scold her for leaving without talking to them first. And she deserved their wrath. Yes, it was time to go home. She could feel her soul longing for where she belonged.

As they prepared to leave, she glanced at the peaceful moving river. "Shame the river won't take us to Fort Worth."

"Yeah, it is. We'd be there in a day, instead of several. I think we can make it in two." He walked over to some dead bushes and moved them aside. Shoving rocks out of the way, he reached down and pulled out a bank bag.

"Oh, my God. I almost forgot about the money," Annabelle said, staring at the bag, knowing there was no way she could ignore or hope or wish or dream Beau was not a bank robber. He was holding proof of his crime in his hand. Her soul bled, despair and sadness causing her stomach to feel queasy.

"Yes, we need to take this with us," he said, holding up the bag, examining the contents.

He stood and walked to his horse, where he put the bag in his saddle pouch.

Now she had to do the hardest thing she'd ever done in her twenty years living on this earth. Beau was an outlaw, a bank-robber, a thief, and she had to turn him in and collect the bounty, so her sisters would no longer have to hunt for criminals.

They would be safe, and together, the three of them could work the farm and live a quiet life. No, it wasn't what she'd dreamed of as a young woman, but sometimes dreams were just that, fanciful creations in your mind, not the reality of life.

"What are you going to do with that money?" she asked, needing to know he hadn't robbed that bank just for the money. Could there possibly be a good reason for him needing the cash?

"You've already asked me that question."

"And you never told me."

"Some things are better left unsaid," he said, pulling his hat low then climbing onto his horse.

She sighed. He wasn't going to tell her, but she knew it couldn't be good. Whatever he had planned in Fort

Worth, he wasn't saying. She climbed onto her horse, ready to ride out for the last part of their journey together.

He gigged his horse, and they started up the embankment of the river, heading in a southeasterly direction. She was no longer frightened, only sad. Sooner or later this journey she'd been on would come to an end, and she'd have to say goodbye to Beau. He'd go to jail, possibly hang. And she'd go home to her sisters with the memory of her adventure.

Only she feared she would be leaving a piece of her heart with Beau. She liked this man, he was good, he was kind, but he was an outlaw. A man who'd robbed banks and roamed with a gang. He wasn't husband material, and she would do good to remember that.

The sun was high in the sky, when the sound of horses' hooves pounded the earth. Quickly, they hid in some trees and brush, hoping they hadn't been seen.

An ache formed in Annabelle's chest at the realization that this was the life she could expect to live if Beau was her husband. The constant running, hiding from the law, hoping no one would catch them. And their children would be tainted by their father's deeds. No, she couldn't live that kind of life.

A posse rode toward them. They were riding hard and fast, and their horses kicked up a cloud of dust, causing a haze to hang over them like an umbrella. Annabelle slipped off her horse to hide in the nearby bushes and watched as they rode past, wondering who they were after.

Beau joined her side, and together they observed the men race by less than ten yards away. Stunned, she spotted Meg and Ruby riding alongside the men.

The sight of her sisters brought tears to her eyes. "Oh, my God," she cried. "It's Meg and Ruby and Zach."

Beau whirled toward her. "Those were your sisters?"

"Yes," she said, trembling.

Beau covered her mouth with his hand. "*Shh.*"

Her sisters rode by, her heart pounding like a racehorse at a full gallop at the sight of them. She wanted to call out, "wait," so badly, yet knew now was not the time. She needed these last days with Beau, because once they reached Fort Worth, he would be gone. Forever.

She would be alone, with only her sisters. She glanced at Beau, her chest wrenching with longing and aching with need for him. She loved Beau Samuel, loved him in spite of his background. Loved him for making certain she remained safe on this trip. Loved him for how he teased her and made her laugh. Loved him for the good man she knew was inside his outlaw persona. And yet she couldn't remain with him.

With tear-filled eyes, she watched her sisters in the distance. Meg's red hair bounced in a braid down her back, her black hat shadowing her eyes. On one side of her rode Zach, the sheriff from Zenith. On the other side Ruby's blonde hair billowed in the wind, her hat low on her head as her body bounced in the saddle.

God, Annabelle loved her sisters so much, and she wanted to reach out to them—to scream and let them know she was here in the bushes, she was fine, and she wanted to go home. But there were things she had to do. One last thing before she could go home.

A tear slipped down her cheek, and she wiped it away.

Beau's hand released her mouth. "Sorry, I was afraid you would call out to them."

184

She shook her head and swallowed her tears, her feelings, and her desires. "No, we've got to get to Fort Worth." Slowly, she stood and stared into his gaze, wondering why he couldn't see the emotion that filled her.

God, she loved this man.

She took a deep breath and released it, trying to calm herself. "Are you ready to go?"

He stared at her, looking at her with tenderness, his eyes conveying he knew she felt torn at seeing her sisters.

She wanted to go to them, but she'd chosen to stay with him, and her decision was ripping her apart. Causing her pain and remorse and a sadness that seemed to grip her in its intensity.

But he didn't know she'd fallen in love with him, and he never would.

He touched her cheek. "Why didn't you call out to them?"

"Your hand was covering my mouth," she said with a flip of her hair as she stared into his eyes defiantly, wanting to pull his mouth to hers and show him her feelings. Instead, she tried to act like nothing had changed, when everything had. "Let's just say I'm going to finish what I started."

Beau shook his head as he climbed back on his horse. His eyes studied her like he didn't believe what she was saying. "We better go before they decide to head back in this direction."

"Yeah. The sooner we get to Fort Worth the better. I need to get home," she said quietly. She pulled her horse to her side and stepped up into the saddle. "Let's go."

*

185

An hour later they hurried down the trail. They were making great time, and as long as the horses held out, they might even arrive sometime late tomorrow. His chest was tight with pain at the realization that soon, they would be parting ways. Soon, she would go home, and he would be back on the trail.

Oh, he knew she thought she was going to turn him in, but he wasn't worried. He knew Annabelle would do what was right when the time came. He knew she would choose him.

What he didn't know was why she'd watched her sisters ride by on the trail and hadn't yelled out. She could have very easily removed his hand, but instead, she'd watched with tears in her eyes. She'd chosen to stay with him and not go home with them.

"Why didn't you yell for your sisters?" he asked again not understanding. Why was she staying with him when she could have left? Was it the money? Or was it something more?

She shrugged. "Like I said, I'm going to see this to the bitter end. I'm staying by your side until we reach Fort Worth. I'll turn you in, and then we'll part ways."

If only he wanted a woman by his side, he would easily choose Annabelle. She was everything he loved about a good woman. She was strong, she defended those she loved, and she was soft as butter in his arms, melting into all the right places. If he were a marrying man, she would be his first choice for a wife, a mother to his children.

But there was his family to consider, his job, his lifestyle, and right now, the bounty on his head.

He smiled. That's what he liked about Annabelle. She was honest to a fault and always told him exactly how things stood. "So you're still planning on turning me in."

"Yes, I am. And I'm going to try to collect on the Harris gang."

He nodded. "I'll do what I can to help you."

Her brows drew together in a frown. "They'll take your word that I killed those men?"

"Don't know. All we can do is try."

They rode in silence for a few minutes, watching the sky as it changed from afternoon into evening, the east filled with shadows as the sun sank into the west.

"How much further do you think we should ride tonight?" she asked.

"As long as possible, so we reach Fort Worth tomorrow. I'd love to take a bath and get a good night's sleep in a hotel bed tomorrow night. Plus, I need to take care of the money."

He wanted to enjoy the luxury of Annabelle in his arms in a bed, not the cold, hard ground. For once he'd like to make love to her surrounded by softness on cotton sheets.

"Hmmm, that sounds nice. And a home cooked meal, sitting at a dining table."

"I think we can arrange that."

"God, I would love to feel some soap and water on my skin."

He grinned and wondered how she'd smell after a fresh bath, how her soft skin would feel. "Now you're talking."

"Wash my hair and change my clothes."

Sure, Annabelle looked grimy from the trail, but she was still a beautiful woman. Seeing her all cleaned up was frightening because he was afraid of how the sight of her beauty would affect him. Would it cause him to trade in his life for a chance with her?

No, Frank and Jesse were too big a danger. If they located him, his life would be hell. They wanted their brother's blood. They wanted him dead.

"We have one more night on the trail together," Beau said, nostalgia gripping his chest making it hurt to breathe. Had they only known each other for over a week, yet it felt like a lifetime. He felt like he could see her brain churning and knew what she would say before she opened her mouth. He felt like he knew her better than anyone else in the world, including her family.

And yet, they had only been together a short while— a short, tense, life-threatening trip filled with danger from bad guys and weather and everything else Texas had to offer. And while he didn't want it to end just yet, he knew it was time. They would soon reach their destination, and they would each go their separate ways.

That was life. That's what happened. With each new day, they would soon forget about each other and the time they rode together. He'd return to his old life, and she would go home to her bounty hunter sisters.

All the attraction they felt at this moment would disappear.

Yet, he knew Annabelle had left a permanent mark on his heart, and he'd never be the same. It was hard to see a future without her by his side.

*

After their evening meal, they sat around the campfire, watching the flames dance an erotic beat.

"Last night," Beau said softly.

"Yeah," she said, staring into the glowing fire. A pop filled the air with sparks, and he watched her shivering from the chill in the air.

"Cold?"

"A little bit," she said, wrapping her arms around her knees, her skirt pulled tight around her legs.

He stood and walked around to her side of the fire. Sinking down to the ground beside her, he pulled her into his body. Knowing their time together was short, he couldn't resist holding her close, feeling her sweet body against his.

"I don't think this is a good idea," she said, glancing up at him.

In the glow of the fire, her sapphire eyes sparkled, and he thought of the afternoon they'd made love down in a root cellar during a tornado. That memory would stay with him forever and he'd never forget how he'd loved the way she made him feel that day. Trusting him and wanting to be in his arms.

How many women ran from him when they learned he was Jesse James' brother? But not Annabelle. The woman had met every challenge head on. She'd faced bats, a tornado, and the Harris gang. Every time, she'd come out more powerful and better than any woman or man he'd ever met. She was so strong, and he wanted her more than his next breath.

"Annabelle, I've never met a woman quite like you. You've changed me."

"But not enough to quit robbing banks."

There were so many things he needed to tell her, but now was not the right time. "Sugar, let's just focus on tonight."

"Beau." Her voice was filled with want. She reached up and ran her finger along his cheek. "I know this is a bad idea, but I'm doing it anyway." She pulled his mouth

189

to hers.

The moment his lips covered hers, he melded her mouth to fit his. His hands gripped her face, and he held her firmly in place, letting his lips savage hers with all the desire he could feel coursing through his body. He wanted Annabelle. He wanted to experience joining with her again. To feel her sweetness surrounding him, enveloping him.

What was it about this woman that made him throw caution to the wind and forget his focus on the job he had to do and the harm his family had done to him?

He couldn't resist her any longer. Lord, he'd tried, but now he had to have her, again.

She wound her arms around his neck, opening her mouth greedily to receive his kiss. He poured his emotions into his lips, letting her feel what he could not say. Her scent flowed around him, filling him, tantalizing him and making him crazy with need. This woman wrung him inside out and left him craving more.

He reached for the buttons on her dress, his hand fumbling, only knowing he needed her, he had to have her, and it had to be now.

She pushed away from him, her breathing harsh. "Stop, let me."

"Thank God," he breathed a sigh of relief with a smile. Together, the two of them undid her dress. When the buttons were undone, he helped her raise the garment over her head.

"When we get to Fort Worth, I'm buying a new dress and soaking this one in the laundry tub for a month."

"You deserve a new dress."

While he shucked his pants and shirt, he watched as she undid her chemise and pulled her pantaloons down.

They stood in front of each other, naked, staring at one another in the firelight.

He'd never had a woman who was so sexually innocent, yet daring and brave. She'd wrapped her hands around his heart, and even now, he could feel it slowly dying with the thought of never seeing her again. He pushed the thought out of his mind, focusing on the here and now and the way she looked tonight.

"I guess the last time we were in such a hurry we didn't slow down long enough to really see each other," he said. "God, you're so beautiful, Annabelle."

"You're not too bad looking yourself."

Annabelle deserved so much more than to be taken on the hard cold ground, but it was the best he had to offer. Even though he longed to be with her in a luxurious bed, right now, he wanted her so badly it wouldn't matter if he had to lay on a bed of nails with her weight pressing down on top of him.

She shivered, and he pulled her into his arms. He touched her with his hands, rubbing her skin, trying to warm her both inside and out.

"Sugar, I need you so badly," he said, next to her ear.

"I can feel just how much you want me," she said, her voice husky. "Quit talking and get on with it."

He chuckled. God, this was what he loved about this woman. She was practical as the day was long and told him in no uncertain terms what she craved. And right now, she fancied him as much as he needed her and that left him starving for her.

He lowered his mouth to hers, accepting her unspoken acknowledgment of the passion that wrapped around them. She moaned and the sound charged through him like a matador in a bullfight.

Lord, he wanted to go slow. To savor each touch, each caress, the feel of her soft satiny skin, but he knew he wouldn't last long. He traced circles around her nipples with his fingertips, feeling them harden beneath his touch. He slid his hand down along her ribs, past her waist, where he pulled her leg over his hip, letting his erection slide along her center.

Though the temptation was strong to plunge into her womanly silkiness, he waited. Her pleasure was more important than his. He wanted her to enjoy this as much as him.

Breaking off their kiss, he laid her down on their bedroll and placed his lips on the puckered tip of her nipple, tenderly sucking the tiny bud. She gasped and arched her back, pushing her chest toward his mouth. He pulled her tight against him, loving the way her pressed flesh felt against his naked skin. All her womanly softness tight against his male hardness.

While his mouth continued lavishing attention to her breast, his hand crept down toward her center. Her skin was so silky smooth, creamy to his touch, and he wanted more. Annabelle filled his empty spaces. She stirred him and soothed him and made him want to be a better man. He wanted to be her man. But that was impossible.

His fingers fondled the springy curls that covered her velvety folds, and she jerked from the intimate brush. His heart pounded in rhythm with this breathing as he stroked her until she was moaning. Stroked her until she was wet with desire for him. Stroked her until she was crying out his name.

"Beau."

Desire raced through his veins at the sound of her voice. He covered her lips once again, raking the inside of her mouth with his tongue, teasing, and dancing, retreating and withdrawing. From the beginning, this woman had tantalized his senses mercilessly, goaded him, vexed him at every turn, and now writhed beneath his touch.

No woman had ever responded so completely, so lovingly.

Reaching down between his legs, she found his hard shaft. As she gripped him in her soft sweet hand, he thought he was going to die. For a moment, he feared he would not be able to control the fierce need that overwhelmed him, causing his blood to race through his veins like a stampede out of control. The touch of her fingers brought him right to the edge.

He couldn't wait another minute to be inside her, to feel her womanly sheath surround him. He moved his body over hers until his manhood lay between the vertex of her thighs.

With a sense of rightness and homecoming, he sank into her body. He gazed into her eyes, dilated with passion, her breathing heavy. Intense tenderness overcame him, and he covered her mouth with his in a kiss that sizzled with the fervor of their lovemaking.

Why did Annabelle affect him like no other woman? Why, with her, did he think of hearth and home and family and a life that was futile for a man like him? Why, with Annabelle, did he feel like his life had been empty until the moment they'd collided in the bank changing his course forever?

That collision was the catalyst that had set his life into a tailspin of emotion and feelings he had no control over.

She matched his thrusts, and he felt the need to

devour her, consume her until they were one. No other woman had ever affected him like Annabelle. Just her mere touch had him reeling with the need to make her his own. To experience over and over this paradise in a world of pain. A world where no matter what he did, either good or bad, no one seemed to understand him, except this woman.

She raked her fingers down his back, sending shivers stampeding through him. Knowing his climax was rushing toward him, he held onto her tightly, trying to absorb her into his skin, knowing she'd branded her soul onto his own.

Annabelle released his lips, a cry escaping her throat like he'd never heard before as her body spasmed with release. The sound of her calling out his name sent his own release ripping through him, shattering him. He shuddered, clinging to her as the world lurched and he knew he'd never be the same.

As the heavens slowly stopped spinning and his breathing began to quiet, he lay on top of her, wishing he could give her everything she wanted but knowing he could not marry her or be the man she needed. He would have to let her go.

Her arms were wrapped around him, holding him like she'd never let him go, and he longed with a fierceness he'd never known before that it was true. He rolled them to their side and pulled the blankets of the bedroll up tight against them. They watched the fire die down, letting their bodies cool, while once again rational thought overcame him.

He wasn't good enough for Annabelle, but he wanted to be. He was a man with a family everyone believed were nothing but outlaws, while she came from the other side of the law. A family of sisters who brought men to justice for the bounty on their head. And they would hang him if they believed he'd harmed their sister.

They would do everything they could to protect Annabelle from a man like himself. While the sex was fantastic, there was no room in their lives for anything permanent. Once they reached Fort Worth, they would have a parting of the way. A parting that would come with the cost of his heart.

Chapter Fourteen

The next day they rode into the town of Fort Worth, and Annabelle felt like her heart would explode from the pain. As they passed the sheriff's office, she wanted to call out to Beau to stop, but the words were stuck in her throat.

The night before he'd asked her to wait until after he'd had a bath, one last meal with her, and a good night's rest. She'd reluctantly agreed, hoping he didn't make her look like a fool.

Now as they rode into town, dusty, trail weary, and tireder than a body should feel, she wondered if she'd made a mistake.

They halted their horses in front of the hotel, and he slid off his saddle. He helped her alight from hers. She gazed at him, drinking in the sight of his handsome face, knowing they only had hours left together. Sadness leeched from her every pore.

They walked into the hotel, and she waited while he signed them in as a married couple. Carrying their saddlebags upstairs, she regretted her decision with each step. She couldn't wait to turn him in because with every moment, it became harder and harder.

She loved this man, wanted to spend the rest of her days with him, but he was an outlaw. A man who had done wrong, when he'd robbed those banks. Yet, she knew he was a good man, worthy of her love. So, what did she do? Her sisters or Beau? Justice or lawlessness?

She groaned as the thoughts spun through her head, like a never ending whirlwind, trying to decide. Sometimes she wished she'd never met him, never followed him because then her heart wouldn't be splintering with each breath.

He opened the door to their hotel room, and she walked through the entrance. In the middle of the room was a double bed, a tub peeked from behind a partial screen, with a chamber pot tucked in the far corner.

She dropped her bags to the ground. A bone chilling tiredness overcame her. She just wanted to crawl into that bed and sleep for hours, but she knew that wasn't possible.

He glanced at her, uneasiness in his expression. "I have to leave for a couple of hours. When I get back, we'll grab some dinner. Then tomorrow you can take me to the sheriff's office and turn me in."

Did he really think she was stupid? "How do I know you're coming back? How do I know you won't go off and leave me in this room, while you head out of town?"

"I promise you I'm coming back. We have some things we need to discuss. Look I'm leaving my saddle here, and I'm only taking the saddlebags with me."

Exhausted, she knew she could never force him to stay, but she didn't like the fact he was leaving.

"I need to run an errand, and I promise as soon as I return and get a bath, then we'll spend the evening together." He brushed a curl away from her face.

His fingertips felt warm, and a shudder of desire rippled through her. She leaned her head against his shoulder. God, how she loved this man, and turning him in was twisting her insides like a wrench, stretching her tighter and tighter.

"Take a bath and rest because I'm not going to let you sleep tonight," he whispered into her ear as she curled her body against his.

She swallowed, pain rising up in her again. He said he was coming back, but would he? And how could she turn in the man she loved for a bounty? But how could she walk away from the money that would finish paying off the farm and let her sisters stay home and not hunt criminals? How could she let the man she loved hang?

Annabelle couldn't turn Beau into the law. She just couldn't. No matter what the consequences, his blood would not be on her hands. She loved Beau; she'd never turn him in.

He leaned back and stared at her, his green eyes questioning, his expression sincere. "Are you okay?"

She smiled and tried to appear happy, when she was dying inside. This journey had been for naught. She'd lost her virginity and her heart and would return home empty handed and heartbroken. "I'm fine. Just tired. You go do what you have to."

He stared at her, questioning, searching her eyes. Then he walked to the door, turned, and gazed at her one more time. "I wish we'd met sooner, Annabelle, before my life went bad."

"Bye, Beau," she said softly as he closed the door.

Pain burst inside her chest like an explosion, almost knocking her to the floor. He wasn't coming back. He was running and that made her choice easier. She wouldn't have to choose between him and her sisters. Though she knew there would have been no choice, her sisters were family. She would have had to let Beau go. Now, she could leave and not look back.

She'd always love him. She could never have turned him into the sheriff. She could never have collected the bounty or been the person responsible for him hanging. This way, he walked out of her life a free man.

Only, she'd be left with a broken heart and possibly a baby growing in her belly.

Glancing around the inside of the hotel room, she realized she couldn't stay here another minute. She was leaving, going home to her sisters where she would be surrounded by their love and comfort.

If only she'd known the misery she was chasing when she left Zenith following Beau. She'd have run back to the farm and her chickens faster than the speediest racehorse.

But to fall in love with the outlaw she was pursuing was the worst possible luck. She glanced around the room. His saddle lay on the floor. Maybe he was coming back.

No, he had enough money to purchase a new saddle. He was gone, and she had to leave too.

She pulled out her little pot of lipstick and smeared the paint across her lips. The time had come for her to go home. Now she was ready to face the journey.

*

Beau glanced back at the hotel; an odd feeling squeezed his chest. Annabelle was not acting her usual feisty self and that concerned him. He walked down the street, hurrying toward the office, knowing this day would bring all kinds of surprises.

His boots rang out on the wooden sidewalk as he turned the corner away from the hotel. Music spilled out into the street as he passed one of the many saloons on Weatherford Street.

Two men with their hands wrapped around each other's neck burst from a window into the street, barely missing Beau.

Fort Worth was a barely controlled town on the edge of the prairie, where cowboys experienced their last taste of liquor and women before heading up the trail to Dodge City to deliver cattle. And many a cowboy over indulged before he went out onto the prairie for six months.

He saw the Pinkerton office and pushed open the door, walking in. A man sat behind the desk. He glanced up, a smile appearing on his face when he saw Beau.

"Agent Samuel, good to see you," he said, rising and stepping out from behind the desk. "I hope you brought back good news."

Beau reached in and pulled out the bank bag. "The Wichita Falls bank job's money and the Harris gang is no more."

"Great work," the man said, slapping him on the back.

Why didn't it feel like great work? His mission was accomplished, and he felt empty as a gutted steer.

"I wish I could tell you I did the work, but actually, a lady named Annabelle McKenzie took the gang out," he said. "She saved my hide."

Quickly, he told John Pinkerton about the killing of the Harris gang, making certain he understood Annabelle had killed the men. "I'd like for her to receive whatever reward is on these men. She could use the money."

"I'll make sure she receives the cash," he said.

"Wait until I tell her I'm an agent," Beau said. "Right now, she thinks I'm an outlaw, and she's ready to turn me in."

John laughed, his voice ringing out in the small office. "Well, you do have an outlaw brother we still haven't caught. You haven't seen him, have you?"

Beau shook his head. "If he finds me, he'll kill me. He hates me that much."

"I'm sorry to hear that. But then, I guess working for us doesn't make your life easy."

"I've been disowned by the family. After the attack on the farmhouse that killed my brother and injured my mother, you guys pretty much destroyed any chance I have of reconciling with them," he said, trying to keep the bitterness from his voice. How did this ass think it'd helped his relationship with his family? They hated him.

The man nodded. "I'm sorry, Beau. Really I am. We didn't know your mother and brother were there. We were trying to flush out James, but it didn't happen."

Beau hated this part of his job. He really hated working for the Pinkertons, and he knew they had only hired him hoping to learn inside information on his brother. But there was nothing to tell. Once he and Jesse had gotten into a fight over Joshiah's murder, their relationship had ended.

Now, Beau was alone.

The image of Annabelle came to mind, and he thought of how she'd changed his life, made it less lonely, yet soon they would be parting ways and it was for the best. With his job, he didn't need to endanger a woman or family.

"I'm sure you want to rest up for a few days, but I've

got another assignment for you. It's down near San Antonio. The bank there would like someone to guard a gold shipment against the Bass gang. He's been hitting a lot of banks, and they need protection for their cargo."

"When?" he asked.

"Not until next week. You've got a few days off before you have to go."

Beau thought of Annabelle back in their room. He could have tonight and part of tomorrow with her before he had to leave. Time enough to tell her the truth. Time to let her know she would be receiving the bounty on the Harris gang.

"I'll take the job." It would be a good excuse to give Annabelle and send her home.

"Great. I'll wire them. And great job on the Harris gang. That's one less set of thugs we have to worry about."

"Thanks, John. I'll leave the day after tomorrow."

Beau walked out the door of the office. Now he wanted to get a haircut and look for something to give Annabelle. The woman didn't have any fancy trinkets. He wanted to give her something to remind her of him.

That uneasy feeling returned when he thought about Annabelle. The woman had wrapped her hands around his heart. He couldn't wait to get back to the hotel and spend time with her.

*

Annabelle mounted her horse and turned toward Zenith. Tears welled up in her eyes as she headed for home. She longed to locate her sisters, to reach home, her farm and her chickens. Maybe she'd find her sisters searching for her on the way. Regardless, the trail ahead would be long and lonely. No more bounty hunting for her, she was done .

She'd packed her saddlebags with food and water and wore her six-shooter low on her hips and easily attainable. Any smart individual would reconsider harassing her right now. Hurt and angry enough, she'd be tempted to kill the first person who thought about messing with her. Life had dealt her a blow, and she just wanted to get home and let the familiar surroundings soothe her battered soul.

Riding through town at almost noon, she passed several saloons that had music blasting out into the street and were filled with rowdy men. This town was as wild as any she'd ever been to, and poor Zenith looked boring compared to the riotous streets of Fort Worth.

She just wanted to get out of here before Beau spotted her or some randy cowboy thought she was available.

Not that she expected Beau to find her. He was probably on his way out of town by now to escape the noose that waited for him. But she didn't know if she could see him without catapulting into his arms and riding away with him. The best thing for her was to leave without facing him.

She kept her hat pulled low over her face, her head tilted to where she could see the road out of town. She wanted to put as many miles as possible behind her this afternoon, to get out of Fort Worth and away from Beau Samuel. She doubted he would be looking for her, but she needed distance between them right now.

At the edge of town, she breathed a sigh of relief and gigged her horse. With her heart shattered, tears of relief and sadness flowed unchecked down her cheeks. She was going home.

"Annabelle!" Someone yelled, and her heart leaped into her throat. She recognized that voice. She knew that person.

She whirled around.

Racing toward her on their horses were her sisters and Zach. They pulled to a stop and jumped down from their mounts. She leaped off her horse and threw her arms around Meg, who'd reached her first.

The feel of her sister's soft body wrapping her in an embrace filled Annabelle's aching heart with joy and relief. She needed the comforting embrace of her sisters.

"Annabelle," Meg said, hugging her tightly. "We've been so worried. Where have you been?"

Tears welled up in her eyes, and she started to blubber like a whale in mating season. "Meg, oh, Meg. I did something really bad."

Ruby pushed Zach out of the way and surrounded Annabelle, her arms coming around both of her sisters. "Shh... It's okay, Annabelle. We've got you now."

She'd never been so glad to see Meg and Ruby. She'd missed them more than her next breath. "I want to go home. Please take me home," she wailed in her sisters' arms.

"What happened, Annabelle?" Meg asked. "If someone hurt you, I'll kill him myself."

She was crying so hard she couldn't get the words out, but could only sob. She shook her head. "No…leave him be. I fell in love."

Meg cradled Annabelle against her chest and patted her on the back. "Oh, honey."

"Please, I just want to go home."

Ruby shook her head. "Damn, when I learn his name, he's a dead man."

Annabelle gave a little snort. "No, Ruby. I didn't plan on falling in love with him, but I did."

"Why are you upset instead of being happy?" Meg asked. "What did he do to you?"

She glanced at Zach. "He's wanted by the law."

Chapter Fifteen

Beau headed back down the sidewalk to the hotel. He'd gotten a bath, haircut, and a shave. He'd also bought Annabelle a gold heart necklace and a new fancy dress. He'd been gone for most of the afternoon, and he needed to get back to her. Tonight and tomorrow were all the time they had left, and he wanted to be with her as much as possible. He'd even found someone to ride to Zenith with her to make certain she reached home safe and sound. He didn't like the idea of her traveling alone.

Nor did he like the idea of saying goodbye to her either. While he knew it wasn't a good idea for them to continue on, he just hated the thought of never seeing her again. Of never kissing and feeling her sweet little body snug against his own.

Annabelle was the first woman to make him realize how much he missed having a woman in his life. She'd helped him grasp that he was a good man, and she accepted that he wasn't all bad just because his brother was the most wanted criminal in America.

Beau swung open the door to the hotel and took the steps two at a time. He couldn't wait to see her, to spend some time with her, to kiss her sweet mouth and to sink into her womanly body again.

Putting the key in the lock, he opened the door and glanced around. The room was empty. Annabelle was gone.

Like the rising of the sun, it slowly dawned on him. Everything of hers was missing.

His chest felt like it had been ripped open, exploding with pain as despair swept through him. Annabelle was gone.

A note lay on the bed. He shut the door, hurried over, and grabbed the piece of paper.

Dearest Beau,

I had to leave. You may have already left town and may never find this letter, but just in case you returned, I wanted you to know I could not turn you in. After everything we've been through, I've fallen in love with you and knew I couldn't be the person who caused you to hang. I also could never be an outlaw's wife and be in constant fear you would be killed or the law would catch you. I just couldn't do that. So I left and returned home.

Please be careful. I wish you God speed and all my love.

Annabelle

Shock rippled through him like a stampede of cattle pounding the earth. He pulled his hat off and ran his hand through his hair. She loved him regardless of the fact that she believed he was a wanted criminal. She'd loved him enough not to turn him in, even though he'd done nothing wrong. He'd returned here to tell her the truth, but she'd run away before he had the chance.

She loved him—Beau Samuel—without knowing he was an undercover Pinkerton Agent and not the outlaw she believed him to be.

He sank down onto the bed and rested his head in his hands. Part of him knew he should be relieved, but another part wanted her to know he was not an outlaw. He wasn't a wanted man. He was a good man, a Pinkerton agent doing his job. And that job included impersonating a bank robber to catch the Harris gang.

With her help, he had completed his mission and managed to get her the reward money. But Annabelle was gone, and with her disappearance, he felt like she'd taken a chunk of his heart.

*

Two months later, Ruby stood next to her cousin, Caroline McKenzie, and watched Annabelle scatter feed to her chickens, cooing and talking to them in a soothing voice.

"Something's wrong with her," Caroline said. "She's not been right in the head since she returned."

Caroline was right. Annabelle had changed since she'd returned. Sure, she was her same stubborn, determined self, but she reeked of sadness, and Ruby often heard her sister crying at night. Ruby would like to hunt down the man who'd done this to her sister, but Annabelle wouldn't even mention his name.

"I know. She refuses to talk about what happened or even tell us which outlaw she tried to bring in. Every time Meg and Zach come out to check on her, she won't tell Meg or myself anything," Ruby said. She lined up the cans on the fence post, taking aim with her Baby Dragoon pistol.

"Do you think she was raped?" Caroline asked.

"Meg asked her and she said no," Ruby said, watching her sister. "In fact, she laughed and got kind of hysterical. Then she asked Meg if Zach had raped her? I thought the two of them were going to get into fisticuffs over that remark."

Ruby raised her arm, steadied her hand as she aimed at a tin can, then squeezed the trigger, hitting it in the center and sending it flying off the fence post.

"Part of me thinks I should stay here and watch over her, but I really want to go hunting again. I miss it," she said with a sigh.

"I want to go with you," Caroline said, her voice soft. "I want to see for myself if I can bring in a bad man. I want to tie him up and make him pay for whatever he's done."

Ruby whipped around and gazed at her cousin. A laugh rumbled from Ruby's chest. "You're not going anywhere with me until you learn to shoot. You're not accidentally shooting me because you don't know how to use a gun."

Caroline planted her hands on her hips and pouted her bottom lip. "That's why I'm here. You were going to show me how to handle a gun. I even went to the mercantile and bought me a six shooter." She laughed. "I told old man Smith I was buying it as a gift."

"You want to go bounty hunting with me?" Ruby asked shocked.

"Yes," her cousin said, her hazel eyes dancing with merriment.

"Have you told your mama you're going hunting?" Ruby asked.

Caroline took a deep breath. "Not yet. There's no sense in stirring up the pot until I learn how to shoot. Once I'm good with a gun, then I'll tell Mama, but she's going to be mad enough to eat the Devil with his horns on."

"You have to tell her," Ruby said. "I don't want her worrying about you like we worried about Annabelle. It was terrible."

"You're right. But I've got to go. She invited Jimmy Brown, the hog farmer, to the house for dinner. She thinks he'd be a good husband for me. That man stinks. I'm not marrying a stinky hog farmer." Caroline shook her head, crossing her arms over her chest.

"So why do you want to go with me?" Ruby asked. "What's in it for you?"

"I reckon I can learn to take care of myself. Not be dependent on my mother or anyone. If I can earn money, I won't need them," she said, with a defiant snap of her head, her voice so soft Ruby had to listen carefully to hear her.

"You're going to have to toughen up if you're going with me. You're as soft as a goose-hair pillow."

"I know. That's why I'm here to learn from you," Caroline said. "I'd be right honored for you to teach me what you know. Then we can hit the trail, you and me, the petticoat avengers, bringing justice to the prairie."

Ruby stared at her cousin and shook her head. She really didn't believe Caroline was tough enough to become a bounty hunter, but the sting operations went down better with two working together. And Ruby had no one to help her now that Meg had retired.

"Can you become defiant in your attitude? Men, especially outlaws, should fear your name."

Caroline thought for a moment. "I think I can make them fear me."

Ruby must be crazy to be taking on her soft-spoken, shy cousin, but she was desperate to go hunting and she needed a partner.

"Okay, I'll teach you. When we're out on the trail hunting for bad guys, you need to listen and do exactly what I say. Your life could be in danger if you don't."

Caroline's eyes sparkled with delight, and she brushed her black hair off her shoulders. "I'm ready to prove I'm a capable woman."

Ruby almost laughed. Caroline's voice was so soft she sounded more like a young girl than a woman capable of taking care of herself.

"Oh, no," Caroline said, her eyes widening.

"What?" Ruby asked and whirled in the direction of where Caroline was looking. As Ruby watched, Annabelle leaned over and retched onto the ground.

"Oh, my," Caroline said. "That's the second time today she's not kept her food down."

"I know. She's been feeling poorly now for over a month. I keep trying to get her to go to the doctor, but she refuses," Ruby said, worried about Annabelle.

Annabelle straightened up and put the back of her hand to her forehead.

Ruby walked toward her. "You all right?"

"I'm fine."

"You're pale and shaking. The chickens are fed. Go lay down for a little while. I'll put them up before dark."

Tears sprang into Annabelle's eyes. "Thanks, Ruby. Please don't tell Meg I've been feeling poorly. It's going to be all right."

Ruby frowned. "I'm worried about you."

"Don't be," Annabelle responded. "When are you leaving? I know you and Caroline have been over there whispering. When do you plan to go hunting again?"

"Not for a while. Caroline wants to go with me, and I

need to train her how to use a gun. I'm not taking a woman with me who can't shoot."

Annabelle smiled. "We were lucky our papa taught us so much."

"Yes, we were. Now, you go rest, and Caroline and I are going to shoot some tin cans. Unless, you'd like to join us. You always were good at hitting a can."

Annabelle reached out and placed her hand on Ruby's arm. "No, I need to rest. But would you put up a can for me and draw a dark haired man with emerald eyes?"

Ruby smiled. "Will do. And I'll make certain he gets one right between those green eyes."

"Thanks," Annabelle said with a sigh and strolled toward the house.

Caroline walked up to Ruby. "Is she all right?"

"She says she is, but I'd give anything to find the man who did this to her. I'd like to show him when you mess with one McKenzie sister, you get all of us."

"She won't tell you his name?"

"No, said she didn't want anything to happen to him. She knows we'd be hunting him with a vengeance, and he'd be swinging from a rope."

*

Beau rode beside the wagon that could be loaded with a box of gold and money from the San Antonio Bank and Loan Company. It was his job to escort the money to Austin, but the bank was sending out three different shipments in three different directions, and none of the parties involved knew if they were carrying the actual goods or if they were traveling with a decoy.

Either way, their lives were on the line protecting the cargo, but Beau had a hard time staying focused. This was his third trip for the bank since Annabelle had deserted him in Fort Worth.

At first he'd felt a sense of relief, then anger. Now, damn it, now all he could do was think about the buxomly blonde. He missed her. His chest ached at the memory of her violet flashing eyes, the way she smiled and the way she gave as good as she received. Annabelle was a woman who let him know exactly how she felt. And he liked that about her.

She'd made him realize he was a good man who deserved the love of a woman and a family. His own family had sent him packing, but that didn't mean that he couldn't have a wife and kids, did it? Annabelle was his family, and she'd made him feel loved and special, and God, how he missed her.

In a thousand years, he'd never imagined himself falling in love. But she'd captured his heart and now all he could do was think about her, instead of focusing on the job he'd once found enjoyable. The job that proved he was a good, honest man, not an outlaw.

But since Annabelle had charged into his life, he loathed this job. She helped him realize he was a good man regardless of his family. He no longer needed this job to prove his self worth.

The Pinkerton's had used him, and he'd known it all along. Using them back, he now longed for something different. He wanted to return to his roots and maybe start a farm. Raise some cattle and pigs and even a few chickens.

This life of riding the trail, either protecting or searching for someone, had grown old. He'd reached an age when he no longer wanted to show the world he wasn't like his brother or his family. He no longer had to prove to anyone who he was.

He knew exactly who he was and he didn't need to prove anything to anyone.

He wanted to be Annabelle's man.

As soon as they reached Austin, he'd made up his mind. He would telegraph the Pinkerton office in Fort Worth and tell John he was done.

Finished. He was resigning from the Pinkertons.

The image of Annabelle floated in his mind, and he sighed. He needed her by his side. He needed to find Annabelle, and if she'd accept him, he wanted to be her husband. To promise her forever. To love that sassy-mouthed woman from now until the end of time.

This was no longer the life for him, and instead, he wanted the two of them to begin their life together, either on her farm or by starting another farm. It didn't matter to him as long as she was by his side.

Jesse and Frank might find him and kill him, but until they did, he wanted to be Annabelle's man. He needed her to know she was all that mattered and she'd branded her initials on his heart.

Shots rang out—the signal from the scouts that there were riders about.

Beau glanced around the countryside, anxiously searching for what had drawn his man's gunfire. He was going to get killed if he didn't get his mind off of Annabelle.

He located the riders on the hill. "We've got company, gentlemen."

Beau's men picked up their speed, and he watched as the riders sat on their horses, gazing at them from a distance. Hopefully, they wouldn't follow. But his gun was out, his men alerted, and they were prepared.

In another hour, they'd reach Austin, and then he could go after the woman he loved.

*

Annabelle had made a decision. She couldn't go any longer without talking to Beau. She had to find him. She had to speak to him. It had been two long months since she'd seen him. She couldn't eat, she couldn't sleep, and she couldn't wait any longer.

Soon, everyone would know.

In the deepest recesses of her heart, she'd hoped he would come for her. But that wasn't happening.

The sun had risen; she'd fed the chickens and done as many chores as she could. Now she was leaving. She grabbed her saddlebags and walked out the door, glancing back one last time, uncertain she would ever return.

She wasn't going to tell Ruby until right before she left. This way she'd have a shorter time period of having to listen to Ruby pitch a fit over Annabelle leaving.

Ever since Annabelle had gone after Beau, they'd been watching her like a hawk. And she was sick to death of them treating her like she was about to break.

She took a deep breath and sighed. She *was* about to break. She felt like a piece of fine china; if you tipped her over, she'd shatter.

She walked to the barn and saddled her horse. Tying the cinch on tight, she had no clue where to begin to locate Beau. If she had to, she'd go to Missouri and find his family, but she was hoping it wouldn't come to that. She was hoping he was still right where she'd left him in Fort Worth.

And that's where she was headed. The wild, wooly city of Fort Worth, Texas.

215

The barn door opened and Ruby came inside, wiping the sweat from her forehead. "Summer has arrived, and it's already getting hot this morning."

Her eyes widened as she stared at Annabelle. "What are you doing? Where are you going?"

Annabelle licked her lips. "I can't do this anymore. I have to talk to him. I've got to find Beau."

For two months she'd tried to banish him from her heart and soul, but his presence seemed even stronger now. Her chest ached with sadness and longing, and God, she hoped he would have her. She'd leave everything behind just to spend time with her outlaw lover.

"Like hell," Ruby said. "Have you lost your mind?"

"Yes, I think I have," Annabelle replied, raising her voice. "I can't sleep, I can't eat, I dream about him. I can't live without him. I've got to find him and talk to him, tell him…"

There were so many things she needed to tell him. So many things about their time together that she'd looked back on and thought he was too good a man to be an outlaw. But that bank bag had been clear evidence he was a criminal.

Ruby frowned at her sister. "You're not leaving without me riding with you."

"You need to stay here. You're training Caroline, and the two of you are going hunting soon."

Who would take care of the farm with everyone but Meg gone? Annabelle's beloved chickens would have no one to look out for them, but they would find someone to feed them. Her place was with Beau, not here.

"No, you're not going alone. Let me grab my things, and we'll do this together. This is what got you into trouble to begin with. You tried to go on your own."

Annabelle sniffed. "I know. But I've got to find him, and I didn't want to ask you to go with me. And Meg…she's happily married."

"Annabelle, we'll do this. It's okay. We'll find Beau."

"Thanks, Ruby," she said. Maybe it would be better to have another person along. Especially as poorly as Annabelle had felt in the last few months.

"I'll run to the house and pack a quick bag. Wait for me."

"I will," Annabelle said. She loaded her belongings into the saddlebags. Today, she knew how to take care of herself on the trail, but that day she'd followed Beau out of town she'd been such a greenhorn is so many ways. No more.

She pulled her horse through the door of the barn and almost ran smack dab into a man.

"Slow down. There's still plenty of cash in the bank."

Oh, my God. It was Beau.

Her heart leaped into her throat and tears welled up in her eyes. Dang, but she cried so easily now. He repeated the very words he'd said to her when they'd collided the first day. She stepped back and gazed into his emerald eyes. She could smell the familiar scent of soap and a campfire.

"Beau," she cried, staring at him in surprise. "What…what are you doing here?"

"Annabelle," he said, his voice rough, his green eyes warm. "I came to talk to you. I had to find you."

"But the law, won't they be after you? We need to go, my brother-in-law is a sheriff," she said, glancing around like Zach would come out at any second. She had to get Beau out of here before her sisters realized who he was and turned him in for the bounty. They would too, just because they knew how this man had left her so fragile.

"It's okay. I'm not really an outlaw," he said, reaching out and touching her cheek. "You left before I could come back and tell you the truth. I'm not wanted. I was a Pinkerton agent."

She licked her lips and stared at him. She couldn't believe what she was hearing. "But that wanted poster? It showed you were a bank robber." *He wasn't an outlaw? He wasn't wanted by the law?*

"We did that so the outlaws would believe I was wanted just like them. It was all a lie so they would accept me into their gang. The Harris gang."

A spark of anger zinged down her spine. "Are you telling me you let me believe you were an outlaw the entire time we were together when you weren't? My God! Didn't you think I deserved the truth?"

She'd agonized over the fact she had to turn him in, and now he was telling her it had all been one big ruse to catch criminals? She wanted to kick him, yet it was so good to see him.

"I'm afraid so, sugar. I couldn't tell you until after we reached Fort Worth and I handed in the money from the bank. Then I could tell you," he said, a smile turning up the corner of his mouth. His hands reached out for her. "But when I returned to the hotel, you were gone."

She doubled up her fist and hit him in the arm. "Gosh, darn it, Beau Samuel. You lied to me. I was so torn between turning you in and you hanging and my family. I've been all busted up inside, fearing I'd made the wrong decision."

He ran a finger down her cheek. "I'm sorry, but if you'd stayed where I told you, then I would have confessed everything that afternoon."

"And done what? Sent me home, that's what you'd have done. Why are you here now?"

So, he wasn't wanted. Then he better be here for all the right reasons, or she would turn her sisters loose on him and let him suffer the consequences.

Annabelle sighed. No, she wouldn't, though she'd like to.

"I would have given you this." He reached into his pocket and pulled out a roll of one hundred dollar bills.

Annabelle's eyes widened. "What's that for?"

"It's the bounty on the Harris gang and the five hundred dollars reward money I promised you. It's a thousand dollars."

"Really?" She gazed up into his eyes. Was he truly giving her the money for the Harris gang?

He grabbed her hand and put the cash in her palm. "It's yours."

"Oh, my God," she said, looking around. "We did it. We did it. We can pay off the note on the farm."

"There's one more thing," he said.

She watched him take a deep breath, and then he got down on one knee. His emerald eyes gazed up at hers, glistening with tears as he took her hand. Her heart started beating so fast she felt certain she was going to faint.

"Sugar, we had one hell of an adventure together. One that changed me forever. One where I fell in love with you and realized I didn't want to be a Pinkerton man anymore. I want to wake up each morning in your arms with you as my wife. I love you, Annabelle, and I want us to get married, buy a farm, and raise a family. But most of all, I want you by my side until the day I take my last breath. Marry me, Annabelle. Please marry me."

Tears of joy welled up in Annabelle's eyes, and she launched herself into his waiting arms. "Damn it, Beau Samuel, I love you so much. I was on my way to find you. I'd decided I couldn't live without you regardless that I thought you were an outlaw. Yes, I'll be your wife, but you have to promise me one thing."

"What, sugar?"

"I want a proper wedding night, somewhere other than a cold dark root cellar with a tornado whirling overhead. You planted a seed that afternoon—a seed that is growing inside me. In about seven months, we're going to have a child."

A smile brightened his face, and he ran his hand over her belly. Then he stood and pulled her into his arms. "A baby," he said, and she knew he was thinking of the family he'd lost. He laughed. "Sugar, you got it. Whatever makes you happy, it's yours."

She reached up and pulled his lips toward hers. "You make me happy, Beau Samuel. You. I want you in my life as my husband. I love you."

She layered her mouth over his and felt a sense of homecoming overcome her. She had everything she wanted in life—her darling husband-to-be, a baby on the way, her sisters, and her farm with all her chickens.

Life was good.

———————————

Thank You For Reading!

Dear Reader,

I hope you enjoyed ***Dangerous*** as much as I loved writing this story. With Annabelle's story, I took the liberty of giving Jesse James another brother. His mother was married three times and had four children. Two with her first husband and then two with her third husband. In my story, I added Beau, a son by her third husband, Dr. Reuben Samuel. When I read how the Pinkertons threw an incendiary device into the Samuel house, killing nine year-old Archie Samuel, Jesse's half-brother, and blowing off the arm of Zerelda Samuel, Jesse's mother, I had to create a fourth son—a Pinkerton agent. I hope I've shown you Beau's turmoil of how the Pinkertons treated his family while trying to catch his brother. All speculation on my part.

Ruby and Deke's story is next and should be available very soon.

I have one small request. If you're inclined, please leave a review. Whether or not you loved the book or hated it, I'd enjoy your feedback.

Reviews are difficult to obtain and have the power to make or break a book.

If you'd like to learn about my new releases as soon as possible, please sign up for my newsletter at: **http://www.sylviamcdaniel.com/newsletter/**

Reading one of my books is like spending time with me, and I just want to say "Thank you" from the bottom of my heart.

Sincerely,

Sylvia McDaniel

Books By Sylvia McDaniel

Western Historicals
A Hero's Heart

The Burnett Brides Series
The Rancher Takes a Bride
The Outlaw Takes a Bride
The Marshal Takes A Bride
The Christmas Bride

Boxed Set
The Burnett Brides

Lipstick and Lead
Desperate
Deadly
Dangerous
Daring – April 2015
Determined – June 2015
Deceived – August 2015

Southern Historical Romance
A Scarlet Bride

The Cuvier Women
Wronged
Betrayed
Bequiled

Boxed Set

The Cuvier Women

Contemporary Romance
My Sister's Boyfriend
The Wanted Bride
The Relationship Coach

Boxed Set
Kisses, Laughter & Love

Christmas Romance
The Reluctant Santa

Short Sexy Reads
Racy Reunions Series
Paying For the Past
Cupid's Revenge – Coming Soon

Author Bio

Sylvia McDaniel

Sylvia McDaniel is a best-selling, award-winning author of western historical romance and contemporary romance novels. Known for her sweet, funny, family-oriented romances, Sylvia is the author of The Burnett Brides a historical western series, The Cuvier Widows, a Louisiana historical series, Lipstick and Lead, a western historical series and several short contemporary romances.

Former President of the Dallas Area Romance Authors, a member of the Romance Writers of America®, and a member of Novelists Inc, her novel, A Hero's Heart was a 1996 Golden Heart Finalist. Several other books have placed or won in the San Antonio Romance Authors Contest, LERA Contest, and she was a Golden Network Finalist.

Married for nearly twenty years to her best friend,

they have one dachshund that reigns Queen Supreme over the house and a good-looking, grown son who thinks there's no place like home. She loves gardening, hiking, shopping, knitting and football (Cowboys and Bronco's fan), but not necessarily in that order.

Sign up for Sylvia's newsletter at
www.SylviaMcDaniel.com

Visit Sylvia's website at
www.SylviaMcDaniel.com

Follow Sylvia on twitter at
www.twitter.com/SylviaJMcDaniel

Join Sylvia on Facebook at
www.facebook.com/SylviaMcDanielAuthor

Goodreads:https://www.goodreads.com/author/show/150774.Sylvia_McDaniel
You can write to Sylvia at P.O. Box 2542, Coppell, TX 75019 or visit her website.

Daring

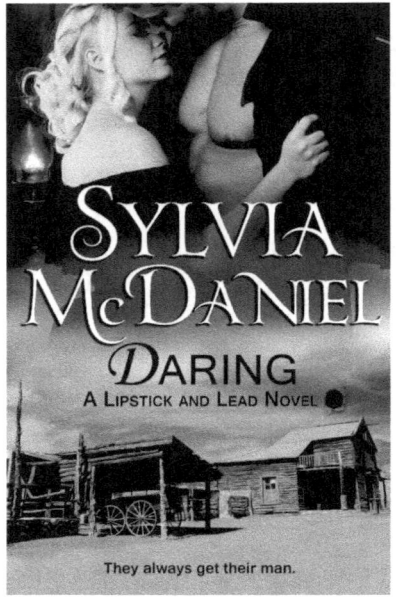

Excerpt:

Chapter One

Ruby McKenzie knelt beside her cousin Caroline in the Texas dirt and gazed down at the campsite. The fire barely glowed in the pre-dawn light. She loved her life. She loved what she did for a living.

"Were you nervous the first time?" Caroline asked her voice soft and trembling.

God, sometimes she just wanted to shake the girl. How could she ever expect men to respect her with a voice more suited for the bedroom? "No. I couldn't wait.

I wanted my first man so bad, I was eager to tackle the job."

Ruby's occupation was a lonely, dangerous one. One she'd learned after her father had died, saddling her and her beloved sisters with a bank note on their farm and no skills to earn a living. So they'd become bounty hunters. Hunting criminals for cash.

"The man laying in front of the fire is the man on the wanted poster," Caroline said, gazing down at the camp below them. "But I don't recognize the other man."

Ruby glanced over at Caroline, her cousin's black as midnight hair was braided down her back, making her look almost like an Indian squaw with her dark coloring. She was beautiful and sophisticated and much too soft for the job. This was her first hunt and Ruby worried, was she ready for the action? The possibility of having to use her gun? Could she protect Ruby in a gunfight?

She sighed and peered down in the darkness trying to discern the features of the second man. "There's no way of knowing who that second man is until we get down there. He could be a bounty we hadn't planned on collecting."

"Or not," Caroline whispered.

"Relax," Ruby said squirming, an itchiness to get started making it hard for her to sit still. She couldn't wait to get down there and snap up another criminal. Maybe even two.

"How are we going to do this?" Caroline asked licking her lips nervously. "It's almost morning. The sun should soon be rising."

"Once we catch them, we're two hours from town. We'll turn them into the sheriff in Dyersville and be on our way," Ruby said pushing back her blonde curls away from her face. Excitement pulsed through her veins as she prepared herself mentally to capture these men. She could hardly wait to slap the rope around their wrists, but maybe that would be better for Caroline to handle. "Let's go over the plan."

Caroline bobbed her head, her eyes large in the moonlight. "What do I do?"

"We're going to walk into their camp with our guns drawn. You tie them up while I hold my gun on them. You've got to be quick before they start to think we're just a couple of women and they try to disarm us. I don't want to shoot our guy, but I will if I have to."

"What kind of knots do I tie? A bow or a square knot? How tight around their wrists? I don't want to hurt them if I don't have too."

The words sent uneasiness flowing through Ruby. Why had her sister, Meg decided now was the time to fall in love and marry the Sheriff? They were great partners and she'd left Ruby stuck with a novice like Caroline. "Just tie a knot that keeps them from getting loose. I'll double check them once you're done."

"Oh," she said biting her lip. "So, we burst into their camp with our guns drawn and tell them, we're bringing them to justice. Then I approach the men and pull their hands back behind their back and tie a rope around their wrists?"

"You're over thinking this. Are you sure you can handle tying them up?"

What if they got into the situation and Caroline froze? How would Ruby be able to save both of them if she got scared?

Caroline inhaled enough air for a battalion of soldiers. "I think so. But what if they grab me? What if they pull their guns on us? What if they shoot at us?"

"Calm down and take a deep breath, Caroline. I don't need you hyperventilating on me."

Ruby watched as Caroline sucked in more leisurely air and released it slowly. She did it several times. "Better. When we charge into camp I will tell them to throw down their weapons. I'll collect the guns while you keep your six-shooter trained on them. Once I have their guns, then I will hold them at gunpoint while you tie them up."

She shook her head. "No. I don't like this. I'll hold the gun on them, while you collect the guns and tie them up. I'm afraid to get too close."

"All right," Ruby said her tone clearly frustrated. But she had to make certain whatever job she gave Caroline could handle. Right now she wasn't certain Caroline wouldn't get them both killed. "You're as nervous as a prostitute in church."

Caroline's body stiffened, placed her hands on her hips and gave Ruby a haughty glare. "Now, Ruby there's no need to get nasty. Don't be using prostitute and church in the same sentence. That's just not nice."

Ruby wanted to roll her eyes, but refrained. Caroline had always been a little uppity. Well in this business, there was no place for airs. Working alone had to be simpler than training this novice. "Concentrate on us getting the bounty."

"Okay," she said taking a deep breath. "Okay. I'll keep my gun trained on the bad guys while you pick up their guns and tie them up."

"Correct. Now let's get going before it gets any lighter."

"Just let me get my horse."

"No, we're walking."

"But what about my mare?" she said her eyes widening like she'd lost her best friend.

Really? She thought Ruby was going to walk all the way to Dyersville? That she would leave their horses behind. The next time she saw Meg, she was going to tell her marriage and motherhood better be well worth the sacrifice.

"You'll come back for the horses."

"Oh. Okay." Caroline stood slowly and glanced around almost like she wanted to run. Like anything would be better than capturing this bounty.

"Come on, after this first time, it'll be a piece of cake. You'll wonder why you were so nervous."

"I hope so. Because right now that pig farmer is starting to look a little better."

"Soon you'll start to enjoy the chase. The rush of excitement you get every time after you catch one of these guys and the sense of gratification when you collect the money. You'll soon love this life as much as I do."

Of course, Annabelle, Ruby's other sister had hated being a bounty hunter. And after she'd chased Beau only to learn he was a Pinkerton Agent, she'd given up the profession. Now, she was expecting her first child.

What was it with her sisters? They went bounty hunting, came home married and soon were pregnant. That would never happen to her.

Ruby watched Caroline shaking her head. "I don't know. Maybe I should have stayed in Zenith and married that pig farmer. At least I wasn't risking life and limb."

"You think not? You would have slowly died from boredom. I'm waiting for the day my sisters come to me and tell me they are bored out of their minds. Men do that to you. Crawl inside your skin and mesmerize you with their soft words and silky lies. You're not going to fall for that."

Ruby couldn't believe her two sisters were married and both expecting babies. Marriage and men, she wanted absolutely nothing to do with either. The taste of men she'd experienced was enough to swear off of them forever. Men were easily deceived, would pay for kisses, assumed the worst about a girl and couldn't be trusted. Nope she wanted nothing to do with the opposite sex, except to bring him into justice and collect the bounty. And she'd do the same if a woman had a price on her head.

"Are you ready," Ruby said rising from the ground. She dusted off the split skirt Meg had fashioned for her. She loved how she could ride like a man, but it looked like a skirt.

"Yes," Caroline said pulling back her shoulders, lifting her head. "I'm going to earn a living on my own without the aid of a husband."

"That's the spirit. We don't need men," Ruby said.

"Especially not a pig farmer," Caroline said her voice whispery soft.

God, if only she could toughen up this woman's image. She talked like she was about to attend a tea party, not haul in a wanted criminal.

End of Excerpt

Deadly

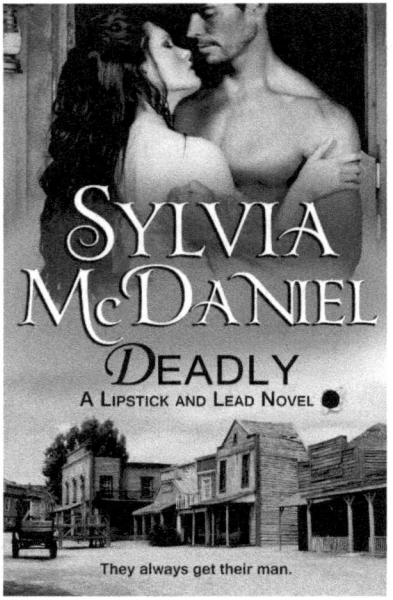

Second Chances at Love Can Be Deadly

Meg McKenzie has been responsible for her sisters since she was twelve when her mother died. While she longs to have a normal life like all young women, she must dress in pants and take on a man's job as a bounty hunter in order to provide for her sisters. In this western historical romance, she has her pistols set on one last bounty to pay off the farm and began to live her dream. But one man stands in her way. One man that can't see past her bounty hunter façade to see the true woman inside.

Sheriff Zach Gillespie has a secret. In the small Texas town of Zenith, there is only one woman who could calf rope his heart. Unfortunately, Meg McKenzie has the opportunity to expose his secret to the world. In the past, she'd already left him vulnerable, naked, and tied up and now she's on the prowl again. He must choose what kind of man he is, a law-abiding sheriff or an on the run outlaw. Will her belief in him lead him down the right path? Will she give him a second chance to show he's the only man for her?

The Rancher Takes a Bride

In Fort Worth, Texas, Rose Severin, runs a seance parlor where she speaks to the dead or at least she pretends to until she can earn enough money to get out of this cowboy town and become a famous actress like her mother. Travis Burnett is resolved to rid the western town of imposters like Rose. But Eugenia thinks the fiery Rose is just the woman for her obstinate son. She schemes to keep Rose at the family ranch where Travis soon realizes that the supposed spiritualist is more than just a pretty swindler.

www.ingramcontent.com/pod-product-compliance
Lightning Source LLC
Chambersburg PA
CBHW071148170626
46809CB00002B/823